FRACTURED MEMORIES

BADGE OF HONOR SERIES

LYNN SHANNON

FRACTURED MEMORIES

When I am afraid, I put my trust in you. In God, whose
word I praise

Psalm 56:3-4

ONE

A twig snapped.

Texas Ranger Felicity Capshaw paused midstep. Humid air wrapped around her like a damp blanket. Despite the warm temperatures, goose bumps broke out across her skin. She had the faintest impression someone was lurking in the woods.

Watching.

Her fingers brushed against the weapon secured at her hip. Held her breath. Dusk painted the sky with deep blues and purples as the afternoon gave way to evening.

An animal darted out from the brush and skirted across the path. A raccoon. Or a rabbit. It was too dark to tell in the waning sunlight.

Felicity let out the breath she was holding. Normally, she would've laughed at her overreaction, but not today. Her emotions were too raw. Every nerve was strung tight and had been since she'd arrived in Knoxville this afternoon. The quiet Texas town was quaint, with red-brick buildings and country living appeal. But she knew that evil lurked under the gentile veneer. She'd seen it. Been within a breath of it.

The lights from her rented lake house beckoned like a beacon of safety. She should go inside and stop with this foolish errand. Memories weren't like lightning strikes. She couldn't hope to hold up a metal rod and have one snap into her mind. Especially since this wasn't her first trip to Knoxville. She'd visited her hometown several times since becoming a ranger to work cases alongside the dedicated police officers sworn to protect the residents. But this time, things were different.

This case was personal.

Fifteen years ago, on a hot summer night much like this one, Felicity's babysitter was murdered. Brooke Peterson was shot by an unknown assailant late in the evening. It was a crime Felicity witnessed, at least in part, but had no memory of. She'd been found by the police hiding in the guest bedroom closet. The killer never caught.

Nightmares stalked Felicity afterward. Shadowy and terrifying, she'd wake up screaming in a pool of sweat. In a desperate attempt to provide relief, her father packed them up six months after the crime and moved them across the state for a fresh start. It'd helped. For a while. But safety was an illusion, and the nightmares continued to haunt her. Nothing could fully erase the sense of guilt and responsibility hanging around her neck like an anvil. A weight that grew heavier with every passing year as Felicity's career with the state police department grew.

Now, as a Texas Ranger, she had the training and skill to solve Brooke's murder. The anniversary of her death was next week. It was time for answers.

Felicity pulled in a deep breath to settle her rattled nerves. The air was scented with pine and moist earth. Light reflected off the lake's smooth surface, and in the distance, children screamed with delight as they enjoyed the last few moments of swimming before being called in for dinner. A boat motor revved. Felicity watched the amateur fisherman maneuver his dingy across the water. Mosquitos nipped at the bare skin along her arms.

Again, the sense of being spied on washed over her. Felicity peered into the trees and brush, but spotted nothing out of the ordinary. She kept her hand on her holster as Brooke's old house came into view. The porch light glowed, illuminating the yard that swept down to a short dock. Like Felicity's house, the small two-bedroom cabin was a rental. It was empty tonight, and the owner had given permission for Felicity to enter.

Her phone vibrated with an incoming call. Felicity pulled the device from her pocket and glanced at the screen. Detective Noah Hodge. Her former classmate was now a detective with the Knoxville Police Department. He'd supported her request to reopen Brooke's case and had been officially assigned to lead the investigation. Something Felicity was grateful for. Noah was hardworking and dedicated, traits necessary to solve a fifteen-year-old cold case.

She answered the call. "Hey, Noah. What's up?"

"I'm running late." He sounded frustrated. In the

background, a child hollered, followed by the sound of a giant splash. Noah addressed his toddler with a firm but gentle voice. "Harper Marie, this is not a pool. Keep the water inside the bathtub, please."

Felicity smothered a chuckle. She could easily picture Noah's daughter, curls wet, dimples on display, as she rammed her tiny hands into the water to create a huge wave. "Sounds like you have your hands full."

"Bath time has turned into splash time. To keep dry, I'd need a wetsuit and goggles."

"Perfect. I know what to get you for Christmas."

He chuckled, a deep baritone that twisted Felicity's insides in unpleasant ways. She'd always had a soft spot for her childhood friend, but something had shifted in recent months. An unwelcome one-sided attraction that simmered underneath the surface of their relationship. Felicity did her best to shake it off. Noah was a widower who'd made it very clear he wasn't interested in dating or getting married again.

Unavailable men. That was her specialty. Over the years, she'd dated a string of guys, none of whom were interested in commitment or a white picket fence. Felicity hadn't been either. Since joining the state police department, she'd worked hard to prove herself and climb the ranks. And had. She was one of the youngest Texas Rangers in the state, but career achievement had come at a cost. Coming home alone to an empty apartment on her thirtieth birthday left her wondering if it'd been worth it.

She loved her job—Felicity had no intention of giving it up—but she couldn't escape the truth any longer. Life was passing her by. She'd done a terrible job at making room for romance. That had to change. As soon as this case was over, she was taking a long vacation and figuring out what adjustments needed to be made in her personal life.

Leaves rustled behind her. Felicity glanced over her shoulder. The shadows in the woods had deepened, making it more difficult to distinguish clear shapes.

Silence followed.

Felicity shook her head. Nothing threatening was out here. She was just on edge. "Don't worry, Noah. Take your time. I'm at Brooke's old house now, so I'll head inside and look around."

"I'm ten minutes behind you. Just gotta get this munchkin into bed."

They said goodbye, and Felicity hung up. The lapping of the lake against the shore and the cloying scent of damp brush enveloped her. Her boots crunched leaves. The grass was trimmed and perennials wilted by the summer heat were tucked into carefully weeded flower beds. Lights inside the house flicked on, automatically timed to ward off intruders. The back porch was wide with Adirondack chairs perfectly positioned to enjoy the view.

A memory burst in Felicity's mind. Brooke, blonde hair tied back into a ponytail, laughter on her face as she handed over a marshmallow for roasting. The firepit had been portable. S'mores had been one of Felicity's favorite desserts. She hadn't had one in years.

Had they made them on the night Brooke was

murdered? Or was the recollection from another day? She tried to dredge up more from the recesses of her mind, but couldn't. The sick feeling buried in her gut returned. That whole evening was a giant blank.

The screen door creaked open like something out of a horror movie. Felicity punched the correct code into the security panel on the door and the locks snicked open. She braced herself with a deep breath. Then entered the house. Air-conditioning blasted over her skin, cooling the sweat beading along her brow. She shivered.

Her gaze scanned the yard and the woods beyond. No sign of anyone. Her imagination was running away with itself. Maybe it was better that Noah was running late. Felicity would have time to view the house on her own for a few minutes. Hopefully, more memories would surface.

The kitchen had been completely renovated with brand-new cabinets and a granite countertop. Felicity drifted into the living room. The oversized couch and wide-screen television were modern. Large floor-to-ceiling windows overlooked the lake. Tile had replaced the carpet. Felicity stood in the center of the room and tried to remember the events of that horrible night, but couldn't. The last thing she recalled was doing her home-work with Brooke in the guest bedroom. After that... it was all a blank.

Frustration nipped at her. Locked inside her mind could be a crucial clue that would throw this case wide open. Felicity had little hope visiting the upstairs guest bedroom would jog her recollections loose, but she would try anything.

She climbed the narrow staircase to the landing. Like the downstairs, the upper floor had been renovated with plush carpeting and beige paint. A hallway stretched to a bonus room, often used by families as a playroom. Brooke had used it as an office.

Felicity headed for the third door on the right. The guest bedroom. She ignored the four-poster bed covered in a white duvet. Instead, she focused on the closet.

The door hung open, the inside dark and gaping.

Felicity's heart suddenly pounded against her rib cage. She willed her feet to move forward, but they were frozen in place. Fear gripped her chest, making it hard to draw in a breath, and sweat beaded along her hairline. She had never experienced a panic attack, but from what others had described, this sounded close. She couldn't move. Couldn't force herself to take one step forward to look inside the closet.

A bang came from downstairs. Felicity swallowed a scream as her hand tightened around her weapon. It took two breaths to realize that it was probably Noah coming into the house. She drew in a breath and let it out slowly, forcing her muscles to relax. "Noah, I'm up here."

Her voice came out strong despite the rapid beat of her pulse. Felicity exited the guest room as though the devil himself were on her heels. She hurried down the hall.

Movement out of the corner of her eye caught her attention one second too late.

A set of hands landed on her back and shoved. Pain exploded along Felicity's body as she collided with the staircase. The world spun. Instinctually, she tried to curl into a ball, but was moving too fast, tumbling down the worn steps with increasingly agonizing jolts.

With a final shudder, Felicity landed on the first floor. Every part of her body hurt. Blood seeped into her eyes. She wanted to move, but couldn't coordinate her muscles to work. Stars danced across her vision. Through the haze of her injuries, she felt someone unholster the service weapon from her hip. Then the barrel of a gun pressed against the underside of her chin. A hand twisted in her hair and more pain erupted as the attacker drew her head into an unnatural position and a hot breath whispered over her cheek.

"It was a mistake to start this all up again. You should've left things alone."

TWO

"Read again!"

Noah Hodge inwardly chuckled at the sweet demand his daughter gleefully threw out, along with a wide smile. Dimples winked on her cheeks. Harper was only two, but knew exactly the right way to tug at her daddy's heart-strings. He gently booped her nose with his finger. "Read it again, please."

She giggled. "Please."

He glanced at his watch. Felicity had said to take his time, but Noah was already ten minutes late for their meeting. It was rude to leave her waiting for much longer. He also didn't want to disappoint his daughter. Their bedtime ritual was sacrosanct. Noah worked long and unpredictable hours as a detective. He did everything short of breaking the law to be home in time to bathe Harper and read her a bedtime story.

"I can do it, Cousin Noah," Amber said from the doorway. The teenager was dressed in ripped jeans and a monster T-shirt. Her feet were bare, nails painted a sparkling purple that matched the colored streaks in her dark hair. "Mama Imogene asked me to take over. She said you have an important meeting to get to."

"Auntie Amber." Harper patted the book in Noah's hand with chubby fingers. "Read please."

Noah shot Amber a grateful smile before turning his gaze on his daughter. "Once more, but then it's bedtime." He kissed the riot of curls on the top of her head and then wiggled his fingers in her midsection. Harper collapsed against her pillow with a peal of laughter. "Love you, sweetie."

He rose from his position on the floor next to the toddler bed, ignoring the way his body protested the move with a faint twinge in his back. Noah was getting old. He barely recognized the man in the mirror with the lines around his eyes and gray hair at the temples. The last two years had been incredibly difficult. Losing his wife in childbirth had been devastating. Grappling with his grief while learning how to be a single parent to Harper had been the hardest thing Noah had ever done.

He handed the book to Amber. "Thanks."

She lifted a slender shoulder. "No problem, Cousin Noah."

He wasn't her biological cousin. Noah's aunt, Imogene Garner, had taken in hundreds of kids over the last several decades. Many of them didn't stay with her long due to various circumstances, but there were a dozen who considered her family because she'd raised them. Much as she had with Noah when his parents died. He thanked God daily for his aunt. She'd taken the broken pieces of his heart and glued them back together. Twice. Once after his parents died. Once more after losing his wife.

Shortly after Sally's death, Aunt Imogene insisted Noah and Harper spend Thanksgiving and Christmas with her. They never went back to Fort Worth. A few weeks after New Year, Noah accepted a job with the Knoxville Police Department. Sometime later, he wasn't sure when, Amber began calling him Cousin Noah.

It was touching, and the endearment served as a reminder that families were made. Sometimes by blood. Sometimes by choice. Always by God.

The lilting sound of Amber's voice reading to Harper followed him down the hall. Noah took the stairs two at a time, his footsteps muffled by the carpet. Gospel music poured from the kitchen.

The house had an open floor plan, the kitchen visible from the staircase. Aunt Imogene hummed along with the song. Her thick hair was bound into a braid that hung over one shoulder. An apron, speckled with tomato sauce and flour, covered her T-shirt and long skirt. She was nearly sixty, but showed no signs of slowing down. Along with taking in foster kids, she was active in church and ran the ranch she'd continued after her husband passed away twenty years ago.

Imogen glanced up as he entered the kitchen, a broad smile stretched across her face. "Everything okay?"

"Yes. Thanks for sending up Amber. She's reading one last story to Harper before bed." He opened the closet next to the mudroom. A safe rested on the top shelf. He typed in the security code and removed his gun and holster before strapping them on. "This shouldn't take long."

"Don't you dare walk out of this house without taking Felicity these cookies." Imogen extended a Tupperware packed with homemade Snickerdoodles. "They're her favorite." A shadow crossed her face. "I imagine she'll need a bit of TLC over the next few days. Investigating Brooke's murder will drudge up painful memories for her."

Noah frowned. "Who told you we're investigating Brooke's murder?" That piece of information wasn't public knowledge yet. He wasn't certain they'd make headway given the slim case file.

"About a dozen people in bible study asked me about it this afternoon." She arched her brows. "Haven't you learned by now that nothing stays secret for long? Especially when you involve Maple Jennings."

He groaned. Maple Jennings owned the flower shop in town, as well as Brooke's old house. Noah had requested access to the home this afternoon so he and Felicity could do a walk-through of the crime scene together. "She promised to stay quiet."

"Asking Maple to stay quiet is like requesting a magpie not to sing. It's impossible, and likely added fuel to the fire. I guarantee the moment you walked out of her shop this afternoon, Maple was on the phone to half the town."

Small-town life. It had its benefits and its pitfalls.

Noah took the container of cookies from Imogene before kissing her forehead. "Call me if Harper gives you any trouble."

"That child couldn't be trouble if she tried." She winked.

Noah laughed. He adored Harper with all his heart, but she was rambunctious, opinionated, and stubborn. Under the right circumstances, those traits would serve her well. Under others... well, she could try the patience of a saint. He often wondered what his late wife would think of their daughter. Sally had been quiet and artistic. A deep thinker, firm in her convictions, but with an uncanny ability to understand others. Harper took after her in looks, but the brash attitude was Noah through and through.

The night air was sticky. Milo bolted out of the darkness to greet Noah with enthusiasm. The black Labrador was as rambunctious as Harper. The two of them spent hours playing together. Noah held open the back door so the dog could slip inside. He'd eat dinner, then trot up to Harper's room and sleep on the rug in front of her bed.

Maybe it was silly—Milo wasn't a trained guard dog —but Noah sensed the sweet Lab would protect Harper with his life if need be. Knoxville a safe town, but Noah wasn't ignorant of the dangers his profession caused. Arresting criminals and testifying at their trials created enemies. Keeping his family safe was a constant worry.

He fired up his SUV and steered toward Brooke's old house. The lake sparkled in the moonlight. As his tires ate up the asphalt, his mind turned to the case. Would they be able to identify the killer? It'd been fifteen years. The physical evidence was scant. No murder weapon, no unidentified or unexpected fingerprints in the home, no witnesses besides Felicity. Back then, she'd been a waif. Petite and rail thin with large brown eyes that took up her whole face.

She couldn't remember anything that'd happened on the night of the murder. Traumatic amnesia, the doctors called it. Noah didn't know the ins and outs of how it worked, but whatever memories were trapped in Felicity's mind affected her. The weeks that followed the murder were awful. Felicity jumped at every loud noise. She couldn't sleep. Barely ate. Six months later, her father sent Felicity to live with her grandmother for the summer. He later joined her and the family never came back.

From Noah's perspective, the desperate move had worked. The terrified teenager who'd fled town had morphed into a smart and savvy Texas Ranger. Felicity was one of the best law enforcement officers Noah had ever worked with. She was compassionate and always willing to go the extra mile.

He prayed this case wouldn't be too much for her though. PTSD was a sneaky disease. It could rear its ugly head even after years of dormancy. Felicity was determined to get answers, but Aunt Imogene was right. This wouldn't be easy for her to face.

He hung a right on a two-lane country road leading toward the lake. An unnatural light glowed in the distance. What was that? As Noah grew closer, he suddenly realized what he was looking at. Terror gripped him. His hand tightened on the steering wheel as he flipped on his lights and siren while simultaneously slamming his foot down on the gas. Pulse racing, he radioed into dispatch.

Brooke's old house was on fire.

THREE

Noah's tires screeched as his truck slid to a stop near the blazing house. Neighbors had already gathered in the yard. The light from the flames reflected a mixture of horror and fascination on their faces. Ash and soot floated in the air. His boots ripped across the brown-tipped grass as his gaze flickered from person to person. Felicity wasn't among the crowd.

He stopped a 30-something man with a snake tattoo on his bicep. Noah flashed his badge. "Knoxville Police Department. Did you see what happened?"

"The place just exploded. Must've been a gas leak or something."

An elderly woman nearby held up her cell phone. "I've called for the fire department."

"Did anyone come out of the house?" Noah's tone was sharp, but he could play nice later. Right now, the only thing that mattered was locating Felicity. His gaze skipped between the two individuals. Suddenly, the family resemblance between them was clear. A grand-mother and her grandson.

"No." The younger man shook his head. His eyes widened. "You don't think someone's inside, do you? The place is a vacation rental—"

"You're sure no one came out of the house after the explosion?"

"Absolutely, sir." He pointed to a house down the street. The garage door was open. A motorcycle rested on its side on the concrete and various tools were scattered about. "I was working on my bike when the place went up in flames. Like I said, it was an explosion. I'm sure it's a gas leak or something."

Noah wasn't sure about anything except that the last time he'd spoken to Felicity, she was going inside the vacation rental. His chest squeezed tight at the thought of her dying in that house, fifteen years after she'd witnessed a murder there. Shoving those thoughts and feelings aside, he snapped into battle mode. "Get these neighbors off the yard." Noah raised his voice, along with his badge. "Everyone move to the other side of the street for safety. Now!"

The neighbors began heeding his order. Before the man could leave, Noah grabbed his arm. "What's your name?"

"Jake."

"Jake, I want you to make sure these people get to the other side of the street. When the firefighters arrive, I want you to tell them that Detective Noah Hodge is inside the house conducting a rescue operation. You got that?"

"Yes, sir."

Assured the civilians would be safe until more first responders arrived, Noah spun on his heel and raced for the house. The flames were intense. Heat, coupled with smoke, poured over him. Sweat coated his skin as he circled the property, searching for a point of entry. The kitchen was obliterated, but the west side of the house was untouched by flames. For the moment. Using the butt of his gun, Noah punched a hole through the glass in the primary bedroom window.

"Felicity!" He screamed her name through the opening. No response. Noah knocked out the jagged shards of glass clinging to the frame before launching himself through the broken window. A chunk of glass sliced his arm, more tore at his pants. He ignored it. Felicity was likely injured and unable to flee the house. There was no other explanation. Every second counted.

He wouldn't let her die. He couldn't.

God, give me strength. Guide me to make the right decisions.

Smoke hung heavy in the air. Noah pulled his shirt over his nose and mouth. Quickly, he cleared the adjoining bathroom, verifying no one wasn't inside, before moving toward the living room. "Felicity!"

The roar of the fire was the only response. Tears coursed down his cheeks, his body's natural reaction to the irritants in the air. He frantically blinked to clear the water away.

A gaping hole existed where the kitchen used to be. Flames, fueled by the fresh oxygen, grew by the second. They ate everything in their path. Entering the house and searching for Felicity was against protocol. Noah didn't have the right equipment and should've waited for the firefighters. Harper's face flashed momentarily in his mind. If he died, his little girl would be an orphan.

But if he turned back and later learned he could've saved Felicity... Noah wasn't sure he could live with himself. He pressed forward. The smoke was so thick, Noah couldn't see his hand in front of his face. "Fee!"

The childhood nickname fell from his lips without a second thought. Felicity had played on his swing set, spent Christmases at his house when her father was working, and held his hand at his parents' funeral. She was a part of his life and the thought of losing her was too painful to contemplate. "Fee, answer me."

He tripped over something near the staircase and crashed to the ground. Pain erupted through his body at the bone-jarring impact. Noah gritted his teeth. He turned to untangle his foot from the object. His fingers stumbled over warm skin and silky hair.

Felicity. Noah wiped at his eyes, clearing his vision long enough to assess the situation. She slumped against the staircase with her eyes closed. Thick tape covered her mouth, more secured her body to the railing. His fingers trembled as he pressed a hand to the curve of her throat. Felicity's heartbeat was thready and weak, but there. She was alive. Noah's lungs burned from the smoke even as his mind registered the fact that this fire was no accident. Someone had tried to kill her.

Flames reached the living room curtains. The fabric went up in a whoosh of hot air. A beam in the ceiling groaned in response as the crackling blaze grew larger. The smoke grew thicker. It was heavy and blinding. Noah fumbled with the bindings holding Felicity to the railing. The tape was thick—industrial strength—and difficult to remove. He retrieved a small knife from his pocket and flicked it open.

The house groaned again. The flames were making their way along the roof. Sparks dropped to the ground, eating anything in their path. The couch. The bookshelves. Sweat poured down Noah's face, mixing with the soot coating his skin. The heat was brutal. It stole his breath. The low oxygen levels in his body made him lightheaded. He battled against his own physical need to run. He wouldn't abandon Felicity.

The knife was dull from previous use. Noah had been meaning to sharpen it for weeks, but kept forgetting. Now he was paying for that mistake dearly. He sawed at the tape holding Felicity hostage to the staircase railing. Outside, sirens wailed. The firefighters and other first responders had arrived, but from the way the building was moaning, the roof wouldn't last long. It was about to cave in.

"Come on, come on." His movements were quick, his focus absolute. The sweat from his skin, along with Felicity's, made everything slick. The blade sliced his palm as the handle slipped from his grip. He barely felt the pain.

His adrenaline was in high gear, blocking out everything except the desperate task at hand. Finally, Noah felt the tape give way. He grasped one end with his hand and yanked hard.

The binding snapped.

Felicity's slender form leaned toward him. Noah didn't waste a second. He lifted her into his arms. The house rumbled as an exposed beam crashed into the living room. Sparks peppered Noah's bare arms and burned holes through his clothing. He couldn't breathe. Couldn't see. The roof was about to collapse.

He raced for the rear bedroom, praying they would get out of the house before being burned alive.

FOUR

The next morning, Felicity winced as she assessed the staples along her scalp in the hospital bathroom mirror. The wound was irritated, but there was no sign of infection. She'd been admitted last night for a concussion, along with lung damage caused by smoke inhalation. It would take weeks for the bruises and cuts caused by her tumble down the stairs to heal, but she was alive. God—and Noah—had protected her.

Felicity sent another prayer of thanksgiving upward. She arranged a lock of hair over the staples before gingerly securing her curls into a low ponytail at the base of her neck. Her sepia-colored skin was paler than normal, but cream blush had put a natural flush to her cheeks. She added a bit of the same color to her lips. The result was simple, but effective at hiding the rough night's sleep she'd had.

She exited the bathroom. Her friend, Cassie Hollister, was standing next to the window. The blonde beauty was dressed in a tank top and khaki shorts. One hand cradled the growing baby bump along her midsection as she turned with a smile. "Feeling better?"

"Much." A shower and fresh clothes had gone a long way to making her feel normal. "Thanks for stopping by the rental to get my things. I really appreciate it." Felicity glanced at the doorway. "Where's Noah?"

"He ran home to get cleaned up." Cassie tilted her head toward the glass cutout that provided a view of the nurse's station. Her husband, Nathan, was visible. The former Green Beret leaned against the wall, but his relaxed posture was deceptively casual. His gaze never stopped roaming, looking for any sign of trouble. "Nathan promised to guard your room while Noah was gone." She arched her brows. "If the two men weren't such good friends, I'm not sure Noah would've agreed to it. He refused to leave your side all night."

Felicity remembered. She'd come to inside the ambulance. Noah had been holding her hand, his handsome face covered with soot. She'd lost consciousness again and had woken hours later to find him still standing guard. His protection was the only reason she'd been able to sleep. "He's worried."

"For good reason. You were nearly killed last night." Cassie reached for a takeaway cup resting on the nightstand and handed it to Felicity. Her nose wrinkled. "It's from a vending machine down the hall, but I figured you wouldn't mind. Cops are used to drinking sludge, right?"

Felicity laughed and took the cup. The scent of burned coffee beans hit her nostrils one moment before she took a sip of the dark liquid. Her taste buds revolted against the bitterness. Still, she forced another sip. "Sludge is right. I didn't think anything was worse than police department coffee. I was wrong."

"Maybe I can help." Noah stood in the doorway. Sunlight highlighted the sharp angles of his face and the gray strands woven through his russet hair. A navy polo shirt molded over broad shoulders before being tucked into a set of BDU-style pants. His belt was loaded down with his handgun holster, cuffs, and badge. In one hand, he held a tray of takeaway coffees, along with a bakery bag from a local shop in town.

Felicity's heart rate kicked into higher gear as butterflies flitted in her stomach. "Morning."

"Morning." Noah's lips curved at the corners, creating charming creases around his hazel eyes. He set the bakery bag and coffees on the table tray. "How are you feeling?"

"I'm not 100%, but I'm getting there. The doctor is signing my discharge paperwork as we speak." She accepted the coffee he handed to her without allowing their fingers to brush. Her gaze swept across his face. A faint burn rode the firm line of his jaw, proof of the danger he'd faced while rescuing her. "How are you?"

"Cleaner." He winked.

"You got that right." Nathan ambled into the room and made a beeline for his wife. He wrapped an arm around Cassie and snorted. "Thank goodness you finally agreed to take a shower. You smelled like a chimney." He leaned toward the bakery bag as if trying to peer inside. "Whatcha got there?"

Cassie lightly smacked her husband's chest. "Cut it out. You ate a huge breakfast already this morning."

"That was hours ago. Besides, Noah promised to bring something when he came back." He grinned. "Payment for guard duty."

Felicity smothered a smile at the good-natured teasing between the couple. The love between them was obvious. It was wonderful to see Cassie so happy. She and Nathan had gone through a rough time years ago and broken off their engagement. Then Cassie was stalked. Nathan protected her during the incident and the two had fallen back in love. Felicity had attended their wedding, and now the couple was expecting their first baby.

It seemed all her friends were married with a family these days. Another classmate, Leah Colburn, had also found her own happily-ever-after. She and her husband, Tucker, had recently adopted an adorable little girl. Tucker worked with Noah at the Knoxville Police Department. He was heading up the investigation into the attack on Felicity.

A pang of loneliness struck her. She had a ton of problems on her plate at the moment, and the last thing on her mind should be a relationship, but last night's attack had reinforced her desire to share a life with someone. Not just any person. The right one.

Her gaze flickered to Noah before she forced herself to focus on her coffee. Not him. This attraction to her childhood friend was a leftover remnant of consistently bad choices in her personal life. She was determined to avoid repeating them.

Noah opened the bakery bag. "I've got blueberry scones, lemon poppyseed muffins, and a few cinnamon rolls. Pick your poison."

Cassie turned an unnatural shade of green. She stepped away from the food. "Sorry, guys, I need some fresh air." Her hand cradled her baby bump. "This pregnancy is wreaking havoc on my sense of smell."

"Why don't you both go home?" Felicity set her coffee down to avoid triggering Cassie further. Her friend had struggled with morning sickness well past the first trimester. "You've gone above and beyond by helping this morning. I'll be fine from now on."

"You sure?"

Felicity nodded. "Absolutely."

"Okay." Cassie hugged her gently, careful to avoid irritating Felicity's many bruises. "Call me if you need anything."

"I will." She shooed her friend toward the door. "Now go, before you puke all over my shoes."

Cassie laughed before bustling out of the room, Nathan hot on her heels. The door clicked shut behind them.

An awkward silence settled in the room. Felicity sensed Noah had something to say and was calculating the best way to do it. She didn't want that. One of the best things about their relationship was blunt honesty. She faced him head-on. "Spit it out."

His eyes widened, momentarily surprised by her directness, and then he laughed. "I always forget how well you can read me." Noah sighed. "We have a few things to talk about."

"With the case?"

"Yes." He set his coffee down on the table and edged closer. "For starters, I need to apologize for being late. If I hadn't—"

"No. Don't." She cut him off with a quick slicing motion. "You had no way of knowing I would be attacked. Not to mention, you literally ran into a burning building—against protocol, I might add—to save me. You have absolutely nothing to apologize for. If it wasn't for you..."

She wouldn't be alive. A thick lump formed in her throat, preventing the words from escaping her lips. Tears blurred her vision.

Strong fingers wrapped around her wrist. Noah tugged, and two steps later, she was enveloped in his arms. He hugged her with a fierceness she hadn't expected. The warmth of his embrace slid right through her.

"Thank you, Noah."

"Don't thank me yet. You haven't heard the rest of what I have to say." He gently released her before handing over a napkin for her tears. "Listen, Felicity, it's dangerous for you to remain in town. Let me handle things from here on out. I won't stop working Brooke's case. I'll see it through."

"Noah, there's no one I trust more than you, but I

can't walk away from this." She tossed the napkin on the tray table and squared her shoulders. "It's about doing the right thing for Brooke. I couldn't stand up for her back then, but I can now. Finding her killer is important. I can help."

A pleading note came into her voice, and a tinge of shame followed, but she couldn't bring herself to care. Noah controlled her access to the case. Texas Rangers had to be invited into an investigation. If he locked her out, she wouldn't have a recourse. "Whatever happened that night is locked in my mind. Working the case may help unlock those memories."

"That's precisely what the killer is afraid of." Noah crossed his arms over his broad chest. "Don't you get it, Felicity? This guy won't quit. He'll come for you again."

"I know." Felicity didn't enjoy being on anyone's hit list, but there was nothing she could do about it. She jutted up her chin. "I'm a Texas Ranger, capable of handling myself, and I won't be frightened away from doing my job. This is personal, Noah. I need to finish what I started."

His jaw clenched. Felicity held her breath, waiting, silently praying he wouldn't kick her off the case.

She had to do this.

For Brooke. And for herself.

FIVE

The Knoxville Police Department was a squat red-bricked building with large windows overlooking Main Street. Noah held the main door open for Felicity. One day in the hospital had done wonders for her. Her complexion glowed with youth and vitality. She wore the standard Texas Ranger uniform—a button-up shirt, blazer, and khakis—but on her, the normally stark clothing was feminine. Her curls were tamed into a low ponytail, but one rebellious strand flirted with her dark brown eyes. Confidence and determination rode the line of her narrow shoulders.

Noah was deeply concerned about last night's attack and the potential for more threats on her life. His instinct was to protect, even if it meant going against her wishes. But Felicity was his equal, a woman capable of assessing the risks and making her own decisions. He needed to respect her choices. Even if he disagreed. Even if they made him nervous. It wasn't his place to tell her what to do. The best thing he could do for Felicity was work hard to catch the men responsible for hurting her and put them behind bars.

The squad room smelled like a mixture of burnt coffee and pizza. Cubicles sectioned off work stations comprising a desk, computer, and phone. Some, like Noah's, were assigned. Others operated as floaters for people like Felicity who were assisting on cases. The desk next to his cubicle was free. He stopped in front of it. "You can set up here."

"Great." She set her laptop bag down on the desk. The scent of strawberries tickled his senses. It was her perfume. Or her shampoo. Noah wasn't sure which, but the distracting scent had caught his attention on the ride from the hospital to the station.

Hayley Montgomery, the assistant chief, spotted them. Her dark hair was cut short and mottled scars marred her right hand. She jutted a thumb over her shoulder. "Chief Garcia is in the conference room. He asked me to send y'all in that direction when you arrived."

"Appreciate it." Noah gave her a nod before escorting Felicity around the other desks to the conference room. An oval table and chairs took up most of the space. Sunlight streamed from the small window overlooking the rear parking lot, creating shapes on the whiteboard taking up most of one wall. Someone had attached Brooke's photo with a magnet to the board.

Chief of Police Sam Garcia sat at the head of the table. Deep lines bracketed his mouth and wore grooves along his forehead. Pushing fifty, he had the beginning of a pot belly, but staved it off with regular exercise. His salt-and-pepper hair was cropped short, but thick and full.

Sam wasn't just Noah's boss. He was also his uncle. Their relationship had been his one hesitation about joining the department last year. Mixing family and work could be tricky. Sam treated him fairly, and Noah never took advantage of his connection to the chief, but still... it was a delicate dance that required constant consideration. Favoritism of any kind could undercut Sam's authority.

Seated next to the chief was Officer Tucker Colburn. His uniform was sharply pressed, a cowboy hat resting on the table in front of him. A former Army Ranger, he kept his auburn hair cut close in military fashion. Since joining the department, Noah had worked several cases with Tucker. An easy friendship had formed between the two men based on mutual respect. Tucker was conscientious and hardworking, an excellent cop. His wife, Leah, was good friends with Felicity. They'd gone to school together, along with Cassie.

Texas Ranger Grady West stood next to the whiteboard. Felicity's colleague had worked several cases in Knoxville, and it didn't surprise Noah to discover his presence at the meeting. Company A, led by Lieutenant Vikki Rodriguez, was a tight-knit group. One of their own had been attacked. It wasn't something any of them would stand for.

Everyone stood and greeted each other. Noah didn't miss the way Grady embraced Felicity in a sisterly hug.

The lawman was happily married, with two kids of his own, so there was no romantic interest there. Grady released Felicity and extended his hand to Noah. "Nice to see you again, Detective."

Noah nodded. "Nice to see you too, although I wish it were under different circumstances."

"Agreed." Shadows marred the skin under his eyes, and his jaw sported a five-o'clock shadow. He looked like a man who'd been up all night. Probably had. It would've taken hours for the arson investigator to arrive and for the crime scene unit to process the burned house.

"Let's all sit." Chief Garcia gestured to the chairs around the table. "Ranger West was about to fill us in on what he knows so far about last night's attack."

Grady frowned. "Unfortunately, I have little to share. The arson investigator won't issue a final report for a few days, but has an initial assessment. After pushing Felicity down the stairs and tying her up, the perpetrator broke the gas line leading to the stove and then, using some kind of delayed incendiary device, created an explosion that led to the fire. A witness reported seeing a silver truck fleeing the neighborhood, but didn't glimpse the driver nor did he jot down the license plate."

"What about security cameras?" Noah asked. "Homeowners are using them more and more these days."

"Unfortunately, nothing yet. It's possible the perpetrator hid his truck in the woods near the cabin to avoid driving through the neighborhood streets." Grady nodded toward Felicity. "Ranger Capshaw sensed someone watching her in the woods but dismissed the instinct, believing it was nerves. It's my assessment the killer snuck inside the house after her. He intended to make her death look like an accident. First, he pushed her down the stairs. When that didn't work, he tied her up and caused a natural gas explosion."

Chief Garcia's expression was stone cold. "I don't take kindly to anyone being attacked in my jurisdiction, but it's especially insulting when it's a member of law enforcement. A perpetrator willing to murder a Texas Ranger is a danger to everyone. Are we certain this attack is connected to Brooke Peterson's murder?"

"It's the most logical conclusion." Felicity turned toward the older man. "After the attacker pushed me down the stairs, he said I should've left things alone. I believe he's referring to my request to reopen the investigation."

The chief grunted. "What do we have on the Peterson murder?"

Noah stood. "Not much. The file is pretty thin."

Tucker pushed a closed accordion folder across the table and Noah caught it with one hand. He opened it and laid out several photographs of the crime scene. Brooke lay on the living room floor. Her blonde hair formed a halo around her head. Blood pooled under her body and stained her top. Magazines from the overturned coffee table were scattered around. Her murder had been brutal.

Noah's chest squeezed tight, and he tossed a sympathetic look toward Felicity. She nodded slightly in response, but kept her expression professional and blank. He recognized it as a self-protection mechanism. Knew that underneath that carefully constructed mask, her heart was bleeding just like his was. It was something they shared. A passion to defend the innocent.

"Brooke Peterson." Noah locked away his own emotions, focusing on the task at hand. "Twenty-five. Caucasian. Unmarried, no children. She was shot twice in the chest by an unknown perpetrator nearly fifteen years ago. Her purse was hanging from a hook next to the door and her cell phone was resting on the couch. Robbery wasn't the motive. No sign of sexual assault either. There was no sign of forced entry, so the prevailing theory was that she knew her killer and let him —" Noah paused "—or her, in."

The chief's eyebrows rose. "Is there reason to believe her killer was a woman?"

"An empty glass on the end table contained smeared lipstick marks but no fingerprints." He riffled through the file and found a photograph of the item. "The investigating officer believed it'd been wiped down." He tapped on the picture of Brooke. "She wasn't wearing lipstick at the time of her death. Of course, that doesn't mean much. We have no way of knowing when the glass was placed there."

Felicity drummed her fingers against the table. "Brooke wasn't the best housekeeper. She often left discarded dishes lying around the house for days." She tilted her head. "Is the glass still in evidence? We might be able to pull the lip mark from the rim."

It was a good thought. Lips were as individual as fingerprints and could be used for comparison. It was a shame the initial investigators hadn't considered it.

Noah shook his head. "Afraid not. According to the report, once the chief of police heard there were no fingerprints on the glass, he discarded the item as unnecessary to the investigation." He frowned. "Chief Walters, the former Knoxville PD chief of police, made a lot of mistakes while working cases. Nothing that rose to the level of corruption, but there were several bad calls."

Tucker gaffed. "That's a diplomatic way of putting it."

Chief Garcia held up a hand. "We all know my predecessor didn't do a great job running the department. There's no need to belabor the point. Right now, we need to work with what we have. Keep going, Noah."

"The only fingerprints recovered from the home belonged to Brooke and Felicity." Noah read from a report. "The bullets recovered from Brooke's body were 9mm. She didn't own a handgun, so it's believed the perpetrator brought the weapon with him."

"That indicates the murder was planned." Chief Garcia turned to Felicity. "So why didn't the killer know about you?"

"I wasn't supposed to be there. My dad was an emergency room doctor. On the night of Brooke's murder, there was a pileup on the freeway and he was called in to assist. Dad dropped me off at Brooke's around seven." Her brow wrinkled. "I remember arriving, discussing the need to do my math homework, and then..." She spread her hands. "Everything after that is a blank. From the police reports, I know they found me hiding in an upstairs closet in the guest bedroom."

"Did you often go to Brooke's house unexpectedly?"

"No. My dad had a regular schedule and I was almost sixteen. He'd left me home alone while he was at work, but that night, Dad was worried he'd be roped into staying for a double shift." Felicity's gaze dropped to the crime scene photos, pain vibrating through her voice. "Brooke never complained, never made me feel like I was annoying to hang out with. I know Dad was paying her, but she genuinely seemed to enjoy spending time with me. She treated me like a little sister."

The room grew quiet. Noah had the urge to cross the room and hug Felicity, but that would be unprofessional. Still, it tore his insides to witness her grief.

It seemed Chief Garcia shared the desire to comfort Felicity because he placed a meaty hand on her shoulder and squeezed gently. "Sounds like Brooke was someone special. You have my word that we're going to do everything possible to find her killer. And your attacker."

"Thank you, sir."

The chief turned to Noah. "Any suspects?"

"One. Brooke's half-brother, Daniel Peterson." He pulled out a mugshot of the man from the file and attached it to the whiteboard. Daniel had dirty blonde hair and pitted cheeks. "Daniel has been arrested several times on possession charges and neighbors witnessed a yelling match between him and Brooke a few days before the murder. Police questioned him repeatedly, but Daniel had a rock-solid alibi. He was at work on the night of the murder. Fellow employees confirmed it."

Chief Garcia tilted his head. "Still, it might be a good idea to question him. Where is Daniel now?"

"He lives in town. Daniel's divorced now, with two kids, and is employed as a sanitation worker. His last arrest for possession was one year after Brooke's death. After that, it seems he got sober. He's been out of trouble ever since." Noah pulled out another report and slid it across the table to his boss. "There's another potential suspect we should look into. Kurtis Ferguson."

Grady sat up straighter. "As in judge Kurtis Ferguson? The criminal judge?"

"Yes. According to the initial interviews, Kurtis and Brooke dated briefly but broke up six months before her murder. He stopped by her house earlier in the day to pick up some of his things. Several of Brooke's friends hinted that the relationship was volatile, but no one would outright say so." Noah shrugged. "It could be innocent—people are often unwilling to speak ill of others—or there could be more to Brooke and Kurtis's breakup than initially thought."

"Their relationship was on-and-off, if I remember correctly," Felicity added. "Brooke didn't talk with me about it much, but I know she cared about him. She also had a best friend, Melanie something-or-other. They worked together at the bank."

"Melanie Carpenter," Tucker piped in. "Her family owns the Knoxville Bank. Melanie still works there as the manager. She's also married to Kurtis now. No children."

Felicity's brows arched. "Brooke's ex and her best friend got married? When did they start dating?"

Noah met her gaze. "Right before Brooke's murder. Neither of them have a criminal record, and there's nothing in the case file to indicate either of them were involved. Still, they should be questioned. If for no other reason than to learn what Brooke's life was like in the weeks before her death."

"Okay." Chief Garcia pointed at the case files. "Noah and Felicity, I want you to work Brooke's murder case from scratch. Talk to everyone all over again, starting with her brother, and compare their notes to the original interviews. Let's see what shakes loose."

Noah nodded. The chief's plan was exactly what he'd intended to do before the assault on Felicity. The case file was small, the interview notes severely lacking. By questioning everyone in Brooke's life again, they might uncover a motive for her murder.

"In the meantime, I'd like Grady and Tucker to continue working the assault on Felicity," Chief Garcia continued. "While I know these cases are likely connected, I don't want to risk overlooking something. Felicity was attacked by a man. There's a possibility— because of the glass in Brooke's living room—that she was killed by a woman. We could be dealing with two different perpetrators."

Noah's heart kicked against his ribs. His boss didn't say it, but the clock was ticking. Somewhere, locked in Felicity's memories, was the murderer's identity.

And the killer knew it.

SIX

Felicity stared at a photograph of Judge Kurtis Ferguson. His dark hair was a bit long on the top but trim on the sides. He was closing in on forty-five and had developed lines around his eyes and mouth, but was still ruggedly handsome. When Brooke knew him, Kurtis was a brand-new attorney working in the prosecutor's office. Now he was a criminal judge in state court. He and his wife, Melanie, were frequently in the society column of the newspaper. Felicity flipped through photographs of them at various functions. They were a striking couple. Wealthy, beautiful, and popular.

"Good news." Noah appeared next to her cubicle. "Kurtis returned my phone call. He's working from home today and asked if we could stop by there after we interview Brooke's brother. But we can't delay. He has a charity golf game this afternoon." He glimpsed the photos on Felicity's computer screen. "What are you doing? Researching Kurtis?"

"Yes." She paused, uncertainty wrangling with her need to be completely transparent. "I remember him. We only met once, but Kurtis was a real jerk. Pounded on Brooke's door at three in the morning, yelling about some work event she'd been at. He refused to leave even after he realized I was there. Brooke threatened to call the cops."

"Did she?"

"No. Kurtis left. Looking back on it now, I think he was drunk. Or high. Definitely not okay." Felicity tapped on her notepad. "I did a quick review of the interviews taken after Brooke's death. No one mentions the incident. So unless Brooke told someone—like her best friend—I'm the only one who knows about it."

Noah scraped a hand through his hair. "Considering Melanie is married to Kurtis now, I doubt she'll say anything bad about him." He dropped his hand. "Is there anyone else Brooke was close to? Maybe someone else at the bank?"

"Not that I know of, but her brother may." She glanced at her watch. "Are you ready to head out? Maybe we can catch Daniel at home."

His phone rang. He removed it from his pocket and glanced at the screen. "It's my aunt. Harper likes to call during snack time. Mind if I take this before we go?"

"Of course not." She grinned. Felicity adored Noah's little girl. She never forgot to send gifts for Harper's birthday or Christmas, and on the occasions she could have dinner with Noah's family, Felicity always brought something special for the little girl then too. "As long as you don't mind if I say hi."

He laughed, hit the answer button, and angled the screen so they both could see it. Harper's sweet face appeared. A plastic plate of food sat in front of her and one chubby hand gripped a spoon. "Daddy! I eat." The little girl's gaze shifted to Felicity and her eyes widened. "Fee!"

The old nickname brought a wide smile to Felicity's face. Harper couldn't say her name properly. Noah had taught her to use Felicity's childhood nickname instead. It was rare anyone used it. Not since her dad passed two years ago. She secretly hoped the little girl would always call her Fee. "Hey there, Harper! What are you eating?" She eyed the plate. "Is that applesauce?"

Harper nodded before shoving another bite of food into her mouth.

The phone shifted and Imogene appeared. Noah's aunt beamed, her cheeks bunching with the effort. "I'm glad you're both together. Felicity, I expect you at my house for dinner tonight. I'm making one of your favorite dishes. Fried chicken with all the fixings."

Warmth infused Felicity's insides. "That's kind of you. Of course, I'll be there." She glanced at Noah. "Case permitting."

"Understood." Imogene turned her attention to her nephew. "Harper has been delightful this morning. She helped me go to the grocery store and then we painted lots of pictures. This afternoon, after a nap, we're going to make cookies."

"Cookies!" yelled Harper with her mouth full. She waved her spoon in excitement, throwing bits of applesauce onto the floor. Par for the course with a two-year-old. Messes were expected. Felicity admired the easy way Noah and his aunt handled Harper's enthusiasm. She rarely used an indoor voice when excited, and while they wanted her to be respectful in public, there was more leeway at home.

"That sounds like fun." Joy emanated from Noah's face as he gazed at his daughter. As impossible as it seemed, it made the man even more handsome than he normally was. Felicity couldn't tear her eyes away from him. "I have to go now, but I'll call you later. Love you. Be good."

Harper strained to reach for the phone and Imogene moved it closer. Felicity got a last glimpse of the toddler, her forehead creased with concentration as she hung up the call. A laugh bubbled in her chest. "She loves pushing buttons, huh?"

Noah chuckled. "You have no idea. Last week, she hung up on me and then asked Aunt Imogene to call back so she could hang up again. It took three times before we realized she was doing it on purpose." He shook his head. Exasperation mingled with a fierce love in his voice. "You can't imagine the tantrum that followed when Aunt Imogene refused to give her the phone. That kid has a set of lungs on her and isn't afraid to use them."

Felicity elbowed him in the ribs. "You know... someone else I know has a powerful set of lungs. Remember the time Bobby Jenkins cheated during a baseball game? You gave him a solid piece of your mind. What did your mom call it? A leadership personality."

He nodded. "Yep. I'm in serious trouble. Harper's already running the household and she's only two. I can't imagine what thirteen is going to be like." Noah's gaze grew distant, his attention on something only he could see. "Sometimes, I wish Sally were here to guide me. Parenting is like driving in the dark without headlights, and ninety percent of the time, it feels like I don't have a map as well. I constantly worry that I'm going to screw Harper up."

She placed a hand on his arm, the touch entirely born out of a need to comfort her childhood friend. "I don't have any experience in the parenting department, but from what I've seen, you're doing an amazing job with Harper. Sally would be very proud of you." Felicity's lips curved at the corners. "And I wouldn't worry too much. If you mess up in the parenting department, Imogene will set you straight right quick."

A laugh burst from Noah's lips. "You're right. No one in my family is afraid to speak their mind." His gaze was warm when it swung toward Felicity. "I enjoy having you around, Fee. Maybe you should quit the Rangers and come to work for the police department."

Heat infused her cheeks at the compliment. Noah didn't mean anything romantic by it. The man had just been discussing how much he missed his late wife, for crying out loud, but Felicity couldn't stop the involuntary way her heart quickened. This annoying underlying attraction was getting harder to ignore the more time she spent with him.

She gave him a slight push. "Not a chance, detective. Speaking of work, we should get a move on." Felicity snagged her blazer from the back of her chair. "Let's go."

The sun blazed on the concrete as they hustled across the parking lot to Noah's Tahoe. Knoxville Police Department was displayed in ghost lettering on the side and front. Tinted windows kept the inside several degrees cooler than the outdoors. Noah fired up the engine and strands of Felicity's hair drifted on the blast of hot air shooting out of the vents. She adjusted the flow off her face. "Any chance you can head through the Roasted Beans drive-through on the way? I'm dying for an iced coffee."

"Sure thing." He lifted the console between them, revealing the deep interior cluttered with straws and napkins. "There's some over-the-counter pain meds buried in here if you want a couple."

She shot him a wry smile. "How did you know?"

"You winced when stepping onto the running board and then again when getting into the SUV."

Felicity dug out the bottle of medication and downed two while Noah went through the coffee shop drive-through. Fifteen minutes later, the headache brewing at the back of her neck had been thwarted, and the caffeine running through her system provided a fresh jolt of energy. Noah turned into a run-down neighborhood near a set of old railroad tracks, and she studied the houses as they passed. Many were taken care of beautifully, others were ramshackle.

Daniel Peterson lived in a one-story home at the end of a short street. Woods lined one edge of his property. The lake peeked through the edges of the trees. The mailbox at the end of his drive was crooked, the sidewalk cracked, and an abandoned tire sat in the front yard. Paint peeled from the siding. A top-of-the-line souped-up truck was tucked inside the open garage.

Felicity settled her cowboy hat on her head. "Well, Daniel doesn't care too much about his house but takes great care of his vehicle. Is that the only one registered to him?"

"Yep." Noah joined her on the sidewalk. His gaze swept their immediate surroundings, but the street was quiet. It was a weekday and most people were at work. An elderly neighbor stood in his front yard, watering some rose bushes. He lifted a hand in a wave. Both Felicity and Noah waved back before heading for the front door. "Daniel works the early-morning shift, so he should be home."

He punched the bell. Chimes rang indoors. The blinds were shut tight and there was no movement inside. Noah waited and then knocked on the door directly. "Mr. Peterson, it's the police."

A gunshot erupted in response.

SEVEN

Noah's heart rate skyrocketed as he automatically reached for his weapon while simultaneously searching for the shooter. Nothing on the street stirred. The elderly man they'd waved to earlier had gone inside his house. Another gunshot spilled through the neighborhood. A flock of birds took flight from a copse of trees as a third came in rapid succession. "It's coming from the backyard."

Felicity nodded. She held her own weapon. Together, they circled the side of the house. The backyard was unfenced, providing a clear view of the woods and lake beyond. Using the building for cover, Noah slid to the corner and peeked around.

A man stood inside a small building facing a target. He wore ear protection and goggles. Daniel Peterson. Noah immediately recognized him from the photo on his driver's license. He let go of the breath he was holding and lowered his weapon, glancing at Felicity. "Target practice."

She heaved a relieved sigh and followed his lead by dropping her weapon. Neither of them holstered their guns though and wouldn't until Daniel was unarmed. Noah palmed his badge before stepping away from the shelter of the house just as Daniel set his weapon down and removed his ear protection.

"Mr. Peterson."

Daniel started and whirled around. He was balding, a few dark strands of hair clinging to the shiny scalp, but broad and muscular like a boxer. Sweat stains coated the underarms of his mud-spattered T-shirt. He squinted as if unable to see across the yard because of the sun.

Noah lifted his badge higher. "Knoxville Police Department, sir. Can you please step away from your weapon?"

Daniel's shoulders sagged as he slunk away from the makeshift range. "Who called you guys? That old man at the end of the block? I ain't doing anything illegal." He waved a hand toward the woods. "The county requires ten acres of property before building a shooting range. I have eleven. I'm well within my rights. Mr. Broadshire is just a cranky old hoot with nothing to do."

Noah placed his body between Daniel and the weapon for safety. He holstered his own gun. "No one called us, Mr. Peterson, but I will advise that while you are correct about the acreage requirement, the neighbors can report you for disturbing the peace. It might be wise to move your shooting range deeper onto the property."

"I considered it, but I work long hours and don't wanna have to hike across my land just to do a bit of shooting." Daniel removed his eye protection and hooked the glasses into the collar of his T-shirt. "If you ain't here about the shooting range, then what's the problem?" His gaze flickered to Felicity. She was studying the handgun resting on the table behind Noah. Irritation creased Daniel's bullish features. "Excuse me, ma'am, but I didn't give you the right to look over my things."

Felicity flashed her badge. "Texas Ranger Felicity Capshaw. The weapon is in plain sight, Mr. Peterson. I mean no disrespect. I'm fond of Glocks." She tapped her holster. "It's my preferred gun of choice as well. Although this looks like a Glock 19. Takes 9mm, correct? What kind of ammunition do you use?"

He frowned. "PMC Bronze. It's the best."

Noah didn't take his eyes off Daniel, but his mind raced. The bullets recovered from Brooke had been 9mm. PMC Bronze wasn't what the killer had used, but that meant little. Gun enthusiasts often switched between favorite brands.

Weariness flickered across Daniel's face. "Seriously, what's going on here?" He studied Felicity for a moment. "Capshaw. Isn't that what you said? You used to know my sister, Brooke. She babysat you, right?"

"Yes, sir." Felicity tucked her hands in her pockets in a casual stance. "Brooke is the reason we're there. The Rangers and Knoxville Police Department are teaming up to take another look at her case. We'd like to ask you a few questions, if you don't mind."

Daniel blinked. "You're... you're reopening her case? After all this time? But... why?"

"The killer was never caught," Noah said. "We want to change that."

The older man seemed caught completely off-guard. Surprising. Half the town knew about the case by now, thanks to the flower shop owner, Maple Jennings. By tomorrow, the other half would know. But it made Noah wonder. How could Daniel have attacked Felicity if he didn't know she was in town? Or that the Knoxville PD was looking into Brooke's case?

"Let's get out of the sun." Daniel spun on his heel and marched toward the porch extending from the back of his house. He reached into a cooler and pulled out several bottles of cold water, handing one to Noah and Felicity, before uncapping a third for himself. He drank, draining half of it. "Sorry. I don't mean to be rude." He gestured toward a set of outdoor chairs. "You surprised me. I supposed Brooke's murder was unsolvable. Do you really think you can get the guy who shot her?"

"We're going to do our best." Noah brushed a pine needle from the fabric and sat. A fan above them squealed as it rapidly turned in an attempt to offset the heat. "What can you tell us about the last few weeks of Brooke's life? Don't worry if it doesn't seem important. Sometimes the small things matter."

Daniel wiped sweat from the top of his head with the heel of his hand. "I'm afraid I can't tell you much. Brooke and I were half-siblings. Same father, different mothers. We didn't grow up together and our relationship wasn't deep. At the time of her murder, I was also going through a rough patch. My wife had just filed for divorce and was moving out." His jaw tightened as if he was struggling to hold back his emotions. "It's a shame. Brooke needed me back then, but I didn't have time for her. Now, I could use a sister, but she's gone."

"What do you remember about the night she was murdered?"

"I went to work, like normal. I was working the grave-yard shift at the sanitation plant. Eleven at night till seven in the morning. Came home in the morning and fell asleep. My wife and kids left for the day—school and work—so I was by myself when the officers came pounding on my door to tell me Brooke had been killed."

Noah noted the time Daniel arrived at work and placed a question mark next to it. Brooke was shot around eleven, but that was an educated guess based on reports from neighbors who heard several gunshots that night. Felicity could never pinpoint the time any further because of her traumatic amnesia. It was possible Daniel went to Brooke's house, shot her, and then drove to work.

But why would he? Daniel seemed genuinely distressed by his half-sister's death. So far, Noah didn't get the sense the man was hiding something. "Was anything bothering Brooke in the weeks before her death? Was she stressed about something?"

"She'd recently broken up with her boyfriend, Kurtis." Daniel's nose wrinkled. "Their relationship was back-and-forth. I was glad they called it quits." He took another swig of his water. "Not that I'm one to talk. My marriage ended in a flaming disaster, but that was... never mind. It's not important. Anyway, Brooke mentioned to me she was seeing someone new."

Noah leaned forward. "Who?"

He shrugged. "No idea. She didn't give me a name or any details, just that she was finally ready to move on." Daniel twisted his water bottle and then attempted to straighten it back out again. "Other than that, I think everything with Brooke was fine. She liked her job at the bank." He met Felicity's gaze. "She enjoyed babysitting you and was sad that you were getting too old to be over all the time. Brooke always wanted a little sister. I think you were that for her."

"She was special."

"Yeah, she was." Daniel breathed out. "Listen, I'd better get inside and take a shower. I need to catch some shut-eye before picking up my kids after school. Sorry I couldn't be of more help."

"It's fine." Noah removed a card from his front pocket. "If you think of anything else, call me."

"Will do."

Noah lowered his sunglasses back over his eyes as he stepped into the blazing sunlight. Felicity kept pace beside him. When they reached the driveway, he held open the passenger-side door for before circling around the vehicle and getting inside. "What do you think?"

"I'm not sure. Daniel seemed forthright. He owns a weapon that uses the same caliber of ammo that killed Brooke, but that doesn't mean much. Glock 19s are popular handguns." Felicity settled her own sunglasses on her nose. "I got the impression he wasn't fond of Kurtis."

"Same." Noah backed out of the driveway, heading west toward the lake and the road that would take him to the judge's neighborhood. "You said Kurtis showed up one night, angry and yelling. Would Brooke have let him in the house after that incident?"

"She must have, since he told investigators he was there earlier in the day to pick up his stuff. Daniel confirmed their relationship was on-again-off-again. Maybe Brooke told him she was dating someone else? I've witnessed firsthand how he handles jealousy."

"So let's play that out. Kurtis comes over to pick up his things in the afternoon. He and Brooke discuss their relationship. She informs him there is someone new."

Felicity nodded. "Brooke was shot around eleven. Maybe Kurtis comes back later that night after I'd fallen asleep. He could've convinced her to let him in, maybe by saying that he forgot something else, maybe simply by asking to talk. Then he shoots her."

"It's possible." He tapped his thumb against the steering wheel. "We also have to consider that Brooke's new mysterious boyfriend killed her. Maybe he didn't like the fact that Kurtis was over earlier in the day. Was she in the habit of having boyfriends over after you'd gone to bed?"

"Not that I knew of, but I also wasn't spending as much time with her in the months before her death. Plus, I'd arrived at the house unexpectedly." She shrugged. "Maybe she already had plans to meet with him that night and figured he'd slip in and out while I was asleep. We won't know until we identify this mystery guy. Assuming he actually exists."

"You think Daniel was lying about him?"

"No, but Brooke was smart. Assuming her relationship with Kurtis was as volatile as Daniel claimed, maybe she fabricated the new boyfriend to make it look like she'd moved on."

Noah turned onto a beautiful tree-lined street in a wealthier part of town. The community was gated, and according to the discreet signs posted next to the guard station, sported several swimming pools, a golf course, and children's activities. Kurtis lived at the end of the cul-de-sac in a large ultra-modern house made of textured concrete and oversized windows.

Felicity wrinkled her nose as Noah parked in the circular drive. "Guess money doesn't buy taste."

Noah laughed. "Not your style, huh?"

"There is something cold about it."

Cold was the correct descriptor. Nothing about the home was inviting, and the feeling continued once Felicity stepped inside the marble foyer at the behest of a maid who'd greeted them with a nod. A double glass staircase extended to the second floor. White flowers encased in silver vases were scattered about. Their heady scent threatened to give Noah a headache.

The maid escorted them into a formal living room with silk couches, an electric fireplace, and a view overlooking the golf course. There were no family photos or mementos anywhere. The room could've belonged to anyone. It had no personality. Everything, from the furnishing to the flowers, were shades of white, cream, and silver.

Footsteps against the marble preceded Kurtis Ferguson into the room. He was dressed for the golf course in a blue polo shirt and white pants. His brunette hair was expertly styled and his complexion was tan from a vacation spent in the sun.

Kurtis greeted Felicity first with a handshake. If he recognized her, it wasn't evident from his expression. Was he simply a good actor? Or did he really not know who she was?

The maid bustled in with drinks and then removed herself from the room without a word. Kurtis ignored her presence, shook Noah's hand, and invited them to sit. "Thank you for accommodating my packed schedule, Detective. I'm happy to answer any questions you have about Brooke." A shadow crossed over Kurtis's handsome face. "She was a good person and what happened to her was horrible."

"We appreciate your help, sir." Noah removed a small pad from the inside of his suit pocket. "For starters, can you think of anyone who might've wanted to hurt Brooke?"

Kurtis blew out a breath. "I've been thinking about it since your call... and yes, there is someone."

EIGHT

Shock rippled through Felicity. She held her tongue, letting Kurtis lead the way for the time being. She sensed this realization was a calculated move on his part and wanted to see where it was going. From the way Noah sat quietly, he was thinking the same thing.

"There was a handyman Brooke occasionally used for repairs around her house." Kurtis selected a glass of sparkling water from the tray on the coffee table and sat back in the winged chair. He took a sip. "Jeremy Lara. Back then, he was living with his parents, a few houses down from her. Jeremy had... problems. Mentally. I warned Brooke several times about hiring him, but I think she felt sorry for him." He stared down at his glass of water. "That was Brooke. She always saw the best in people."

Noah glanced at Felicity, and she gave a subtle shake of her head. The name Jeremy Lara wasn't familiar to her, but from the faint crease in his brow, Noah knew the man. He focused back on Kurtis. "Did Jeremy ever threaten Brooke?"

"Not that I know of, but he was mentally unstable. Honestly, I feel bad even mentioning his name to you now. The last thing I want to do is get the man in trouble, but her murder has always weighed on me. She didn't have an enemy in the world, and I can't think of anyone else who'd want to hurt her. Everyone loved Brooke. She was quiet and sensitive."

"It's clear you cared for her deeply. How long did you and Brooke date?"

"On and off for about two years." Kurtis lifted a shoulder. "I was in my late-twenties back then and not concerned with settling down. Brooke wanted to get married. Every once in a while, she'd pressure me about the direction of our relationship, we'd break up, and then a few months later get back together." His gaze grew distant. "I loved her, otherwise I wouldn't have kept going back, but grew tired of our constant merry-go-round. The last time we broke up, it was for good. I made that crystal clear."

Interesting. Kurtis was doing his best to put some distance between himself and Brooke. Once again, Felicity felt like she was being manipulated. The more the man talked, the less she believed him. She kept her tone casual. "Can you remember the last time you spoke to Brooke?"

"On the day of her murder, I went to her house to collect some things I'd left there while we were dating."

He leaned forward, resting his elbow on the arm of the chair. "Jeremy was there, repairing Brooke's gutters. I felt very uncomfortable leaving her alone with him, so we chatted and watched some television until he was done. Once Jeremy left, I did too."

The scenario sounded plausible, but it would be hard to verify. Fifteen years had passed. Neighbors likely wouldn't remember the comings and goings at Brooke's house, especially earlier in the day before her murder. Kurtis also could've come by Brooke's house twice—once to collect his things and another time to murder her.

What was clear is that Brooke wasn't afraid of him. She let him into the house, at least in the afternoon. It was likely she would have again. In fact, it would've been easy for Kurtis to gain access to Brooke's home by claiming he'd left something behind.

Felicity weighed her options and decided to dig for more information. "Brooke's brother says that she was dating someone new. Did she tell you about it?"

Kurtis tilted his head as his gaze turned flint hard. "No. She never mentioned that."

Okay. That question touched a nerve. "Would it have bothered you if she was dating someone else?"

"Not at all. In fact, it would have been ideal. I'd already moved on and was seeing someone new. My wife, Melanie. It would've been better for everyone if Brooke was also happy and in love."

"When did she find out you and Melanie were dating?"

"I told her right before I left her house." He set his

water glass on the tray with a click. "Melanie and I had discussed it beforehand and wanted to make sure we were serious before breaking the news to Brooke. We kept our relationship secret, but we'd been dating for months at that point, and..." He cleared his throat. "Brooke expressed a desire to get back together with me when I came by to pick up my stuff. I didn't feel right about leading her on."

"How did she take the news?"

"She was understandably shocked."

"Just shocked?" Felicity learned forward. "Frankly, sir, if my ex and my best friend started dating, I'd feel betrayed. It would be worse if they kept it a secret from me for months. Surely you must've argued."

"The conversation was... tense." He met Felicity's gaze. "Despite our relationship struggles, I cared deeply for Brooke. It was never my intention to hurt her. The relationship with Melanie was unexpected. For us both. One day, we were just friends and then..." A smile played on his lips. "All of a sudden we were more. It was like a puzzle piece that was missing snapped into place and everything became clear."

Felicity was looking at Kurtis, but she was increasingly aware of Noah seated on the love seat beside her. His thigh was touching hers. Their relationship was rooted in friendship. Based on Kurtis's description, it was possible to know someone for a long time and then suddenly one day see them in a new way. Was that what was happening to her? Maybe this slow-burning attraction she'd been fighting for Noah was more real than she'd initially thought.

She shoved those considerations aside and focused back on Kurtis. "After learning about your relationship with Melanie, did Brooke speak to her?"

His expression once again turned calculated. He was quiet for a long moment. "Unfortunately, they didn't. Brooke was murdered before Melanie had a chance to discuss it with her." The faint click of heels against marble filtered into the room. Kurtis's jaw hardened and his steady gaze flickered back and forth between Felicity and Noah. "I know you both have a job to do, and I'm sure you'll want to speak to my wife, but I request that you keep it brief. Melanie holds a lot of guilt about the way Brooke found out about us. She was quite angry with me for telling her on my own."

Before they could respond, a woman breezed into the room. Melanie. She was tall and slender with shoulder-length blond hair that fell in gentle waves around her sweetheart face. Ruby red lipstick coated her full lips. Felicity and Noah rose to greet her, as did Kurtis.

Melanie drew up short and studied Felicity for a long moment. Shock and then recognition zipped across her features. "Felicity Capshaw? Oh my goodness, look at you."

She crossed the room to embrace Felicity in a gentle hug. Melanie's perfume was sickly sweet, and up close, it was obvious the older woman had used plastic surgery and Botox to ward off aging. Her forehead didn't have a wrinkle on it and her lips were plumper than in her youth.

"I heard a rumor you were in town, but didn't know if it was true." Melanie's gaze drifted to Noah and then Kurtis. The stillness of her facial expression made it difficult to read her internal emotions. She could've been shocked, confused, or playing dumb. "Kurtis, honey, what's going on?"

"Detective Hodge and Ranger Capshaw are here to discuss Brooke's murder. The Knoxville PD is reopening the case." His forehead creased as he waved a hand between Felicity and his wife. "Although, I suppose introductions aren't needed between you two. How do you know each other?"

"Felicity was the little girl that Brooke used to babysit," Melanie said. "Don't you remember?"

Kurtis locked eyes with Felicity and something flashed in the depths of those blue orbs, but before Felicity could determine what, it was gone. He laughed lightly. "Of course. Forgive me, Ranger Capshaw. I'm not good with names or faces."

"That's quite all right." Felicity kept her tone light. "We never officially met when I was younger."

Melanie drifted to her husband's side. She wore an expensive linen suit that played off her bronzed skin. Her diamond necklace and wedding band sparkled in the sunlight. She absently wrapped an arm around Kurtis's waist. "I'm sorry to intrude, but we have plans this afternoon. A golf charity game. Have you asked all the questions you need to?"

Noah stepped forward. "Actually, Mrs. Ferguson, since you were Brooke's best friend, we'd love to ask some additional questions."

"Of course." She smiled politely. "Come by the bank tomorrow morning. I'll be there."

"Appreciate it, ma'am." Noah settled his cowboy hat on his head and then paused. "One last thing, and then we'll get out of your hair. Where were each of you on the night Brooke was murdered?"

Melanie laughed lightly, although her expression held no sign of mirth. "Excuse me, Detective. Are we suspects?"

"It's a routine question, ma'am." Noah shot her a charming smile. "They teach us to ask it in detective school."

The small joke broke the tension in the room. Everyone chuckled.

Kurtis pulled his wife closer. "Melanie and I were together. We had dinner with my mother and then began watching a movie. I'm embarrassed to say we both fell asleep on the couch and didn't wake up until the next morning." He glanced at his watch. "I'm so sorry, but we need to get going. If you think of any other questions, feel free to contact me at my office."

The couple quickly shook Felicity's and Noah's hands. The maid appeared out of nowhere and escorted them from the home. Felicity waited until they were back inside the Tahoe before opening her mouth. "That was interesting. Did Kurtis ever mention Melanie being with him on the night of Brooke's murder in his initial statement?"

"No. You think he's trying to shore up his alibi?"

"Possibly." She cast a glance back at the house. "Or maybe he's trying to shore up hers."

NINE

Noah considered Felicity's observation while driving across town. Could Melanie have been involved in her best friend's death? She'd been dating Kurtis and he'd readily admitted to being at Brooke's house earlier that day. Jealousy could be a powerful motive.

And then there was that pesky lipstick-stained glass on Brooke's end table. He tapped his fingers against the steering wheel. "Did you notice Melanie was wearing red lipstick? It sure looked like the same shade from the glass at Brooke's house." Noah heard his own statement ring in his ears after he'd spoken aloud. "Gosh, that sounds ridiculous, doesn't it? There must be dozens of women in town that wear red lipstick."

He glanced at Felicity. Her lips were gorgeous and rose petal pink. Naturally beautiful. She caught his glance, and those lips curved into a smile. "Yes, red is a common shade. It doesn't mean Melanie killed Brooke. We can't even prove she was at her house. Brooke was also fond of red, although now that I think of it, her color was a more orangey-red."

He tore his gaze away from the woman in the passenger seat and focused back on the country road. What was he doing thinking about Felicity's lips? Sometimes, it felt like an alien had taken over his body. Or at least messed with his brain. "I'm hungry. Are you? I know a great fast-food place near here, although I want you to withhold judgment until you've tasted the food."

Her gaze narrowed. "Is it a taco truck? Because the last time I ate from a taco truck you recommended, I was sick for three days with food poisoning. You know what, maybe I should pick the place for lunch—"

"Calm down. It's not a taco truck." He flipped on his blinker and turned into a gas station. Attached to the building was a hamburger joint. A picnic area next to the lake sat invitingly under the shade of an old oak tree. Moss, hanging from the thick branches, drifted in the breeze. "This is the place. It looks dodgy on the outside, but the food is great. Promise."

Felicity hesitated but then undid her seatbelt. "Okay. Let's do it." She jabbed a finger in his direction. "But if this place makes me sick, you have to take care of me and you never—I mean, never—get to pick where we eat again."

The idea of caring for Felicity when she was sick didn't bother him one bit. In fact, it made him wonder. Who took care of her? A nasty thought worked its way through his mind. Was she dating someone? Felicity hadn't said so, but it wasn't like romantic relationships were something they talked about regularly. The idea of another man holding her close... kissing those lips... it sent a bolt of jealousy straight through Noah.

Okay. He was definitely losing it.

He shoved the vehicle into park and quickly got out, circling around to open the door for Felicity, but she'd already exited and was across the parking lot. He jogged after her. The summer heat was tempered by a soft breeze floating through the air. It ruffled the surface of the lake, creating ripples, while dragonflies darted along the shore. After ordering their meals, Felicity sighed with contentment as she settled at the picnic table. "I'd forgotten just how pretty Knoxville is."

Noah said a quick grace before unwrapping his burger. "Do you miss it?" He hesitated. "Or does the town hold too many unpleasant memories?"

"After Brooke's murder, being here was hard. But now..." She dragged a fry through her ketchup. "I don't feel the same. Honestly, I miss it. I've made friends, but there's something special about being around people who knew you when you were young. You, Cassie, Leah. Y'all remind me of a time when life was easy. Fun. I need that." Her gaze grew distant. "I've been lonely since Dad died. He was my only family."

Noah's chest squeezed tight. He knew what it was like to be an orphan, but at least he'd had Aunt Imogene. Felicity's mom left the family right after she was born and died a year later in a boating accident. Her dad had been the one to raise her. Now with him gone, too, she really was on her own. He didn't want that.

Noah dipped his head until he caught Felicity's gaze. "You always have a home here. Always. Holidays, weekends, birthdays. You can come here. Aunt Imogene celebrates Puppy Day. She'd be over the moon to throw you a party for any reason. Not to mention Cassie and Leah."

She dropped her gaze. "That's nice of you to say, but all of you have families of your own. I don't want to impose."

"Whew. I was hoping you'd say that." Noah shoved a fry in his mouth. "The idea of spending one more Christmas with you makes me want to scream. All those times my parents had you over while your dad was working..." He rolled his eyes. "Very annoying."

She laughed and tossed a fry at his head. "Okay, smart aleck. Thanks for making me sound like Eeyore."

He leaned over. "Well, you lost your tail again." Noah shook his head. "Seriously, Fee, you couldn't be an imposition if you tried. Family isn't determined by blood. It's what we decide it is. You and I... we're not kids anymore, but I consider us family. You'll always have a place here." He wriggled his eyes. "Should we make one of those weird pacts that when we're eighty, we'll help each other to the rocking chairs?"

Felicity shook her head. "When I'm eighty, I'll have no problem getting to my own rocking chair, thank you very much." Her smile was brilliant. "But I wouldn't mind having you sit next to me. Hopefully, by then I'll be deaf and won't have to listen to your complaining. Or suffer through your horrible taste in food." She waved a french fry. "Seriously, you promised this would be good."

"What are you talking about? It's the best burger in three counties." Noah waved over the waiter and ordered half a dozen more meals. Felicity's eyes widened in shock, and he chuckled. "It's not for me. I figured after lunch you'd like to question Jeremy."

"I would. Where is he?"

"He lives in a homeless encampment on the outskirts of Knoxville. I visit from time to time with supplies and food. Kurtis was right, he has mental health issues. Paranoia of some sort. Jeremy refuses medication, choosing instead to self-soothe with alcohol, which is likely why he's homeless. He survives working odd jobs like collecting metal cans for recycling, that kind of thing, and has gotten in trouble a few times for scaring people. In a paranoid state, Jeremy screams and threatens to harm anyone who he believes has crossed him."

"Has he ever gone beyond words?"

"Not to my knowledge." Noah shrugged. "But I can't rule it out. There's always a first time for everything. Kurtis places Jeremy at the house on the day of the murder. It was hours before Brooke was shot, but he could've come back later that evening."

"What about when he's not paranoid?"

"He's harmless."

She bunched the wrapper from her burger into a ball before tossing it into a nearby trash can. "I don't trust Kurtis further than I can throw him. I want to question Jeremy since he was at the house that day, but if what you're saying is true, I have a hard time believing he's responsible for Brooke's murder. Individuals in a paranoid state are disorganized and frantic. It seems unlikely Jeremy would have the presence of mind to bring a gun to Brooke's house, shoot her, and then take the murder weapon with him. Not to mention, if he was paranoid, would she have opened the door?" Felicity frowned. "It doesn't remove him from the suspect list, but unless there's something more, I think blaming the murder on Jeremy is a matter of convenience."

"You're assuming Jeremy was in a paranoid state when Brooke was murdered. He probably wasn't. Back then, Jeremy was living with his parents and while he wasn't stable, things were better than they are now. We can't jump to any conclusions." Noah stood and stretched. Then he collected their trash. "Right now, I'm not ready to remove anyone from the suspect list. Come on. Let's grab some supplies from the gas station."

"What kind of supplies?"

"Along with food, I like to bring water and toiletries to the homeless camp."

Felicity gracefully slid to the end of the picnic table and stood. Noah placed a hand on the small of her back to gently guide her toward his truck. The gesture was gentlemanly, but the moment his palm connected with the soft fabric of her shirt, his pulse kicked into a higher gear. He was drawn to her. There was no doubt about it.

Foolishly, once again, he wondered if she was dating anyone. Noah didn't think so. Her earlier comments about being lonely indicated there wasn't someone special in her life. But what if that wasn't true? It was hard to believe she didn't have a line of men waiting to ask her out.

As if she'd read his thoughts, she peeked at him from beneath thick lashes. "Thanks for lunch. It was nice to take a break and hang by the lake for a while. I hate being stuck in the office and I've eaten one too many meals in a car." She elbowed him playfully. "Even if the picnic bench was by a gas station. Please tell me you do a better job of picking places to eat when you go on dates."

He snorted. "It's been a long time since I've gone on a date. You must be fielding offers left and right though."

"Not as much as you would think. My career has been center stage in my life." She lifted her gaze to meet his and their steps slowed. "Until recently, a good man would've had a hard time getting my attention."

Noah's heart skipped a beat. Continuing this conversation was a terrible idea, but he couldn't stop himself from saying, "Until recently indicates you're ready for a change."

"I am."

He suddenly noticed the proximity of their bodies. One step and he'd have her in his arms. Noah knew he should back up. Move away. But couldn't force his feet to act. The look buried in Felicity's deep brown eyes was memorizing. It was tenderness and admiration tangled with desire. He had the undeniable urge to lean forward and kiss her.

The roar of an engine dragged Noah's attention away from Felicity. A silver truck raced toward the gas station parking lot. He had a single breath to register the open driver-side window, the masked individual, and the sunlight winking off a handgun.

They were standing in the middle of the parking lot, completely exposed. Noah sprang into action.

"Run!" He pushed Felicity toward the shelter of the nearest vehicle while simultaneously reaching for his own holster. The next few seconds were critical.

They were a matter of life and death.

TEN

He wouldn't make it to the SUV.

Noah's mind calculated the distance between him and safety in a flash. He dropped to one knee, held his breath, and fired his weapon at the gunman. The shot pinged against the moving vehicle. Tires squealed as the truck turned into the gas station.

The perpetrator took a shot at Felicity.

She dove for the cement and rolled behind Noah's vehicle. Had she been hit? Injured?

Noah couldn't answer that at the moment. He blocked out any distracting thought and focused on the truck barreling through the gas station parking lot. One man was inside the cab, wearing a ski mask. Noah raised his gun. "Police! Stop!" He couldn't fire at this angle without risking a civilian.

Screams bounced off the concrete as patrons dove for cover. The shooter fired twice more in Felicity's direction before turning his weapon on Noah. Time seemed to slow to milliseconds. The twist of the truck's tires, sunlight bouncing off the chrome sidebar, the darkness of the gun barrel. Noah took aim.

Glass exploded as the truck's rear window shattered into a thousand pieces. The shooter instinctively took cover. Tires squealed as the vehicle raced out of the parking lot and down the street, disappearing in a heartbeat around a bend in the road.

Noah inhaled. He touched his chest, nearly expecting his hand to come away wet with blood. The fabric was dry. His gaze shot to his vehicle. Felicity was crouched behind the side panel, her body raised just enough to shoot her weapon across the hood. With sudden clarity, Noah realized it was Felicity who'd shot out the perpetrator's rear window.

She'd saved his life.

He rose. Felicity's attention locked on him. Her gaze swept across his body, terror giving way to relief as she registered he was unharmed. Something inside Noah twisted sharply at the depth of emotion written in her expression. It reflected his own feelings. Buried instincts he'd battled against since she came to town yesterday. Friendship mixed with attraction. A heady combination that was rare.

It took three strides to close the distance between them. Without thinking, he swept her into his arms. Felicity's embrace matched his intensity. Her body melted against his. She was slender and lush, tough with muscle but soft with curves. A juxtaposition to the hard planes of his chest. Noah's hand cradled the back of her head, his fingers dipping into the silky strands of her hair. She was okay. Unharmed.

The familiar scent of her shampoo enveloped him, and for the first time since seeing the truck barreling toward them, he took a deep breath. Sirens wailed in the distance as first responders headed to the scene. It didn't provide any comfort. The attacker had failed to kill Felicity. Twice.

It was only a matter of time before he tried again.

An hour later, Felicity leaned against the rear bumper of Noah's vehicle. The gas station parking lot was packed with emergency responders. Crime scene technicians had arrived and were currently gathering evidence. The flash of a camera periodically went off. On the other side of the lot, her colleague, Ranger Grady West, spoke with a witness. He'd specifically asked Felicity and Noah to hang around while he did an initial assessment.

She hugged herself tighter. "How much longer do you think this will take? That's the third witness Grady has spoken to." Felicity itched to get moving. Sitting around was giving her way too much time to think. "I'd still like to interview Jeremy today. The faster we work Brooke's case, the quicker we find the man responsible for today's attack."

She needed to find him. Not just for her own safety, but for Noah's too. The gunman had turned his sights on the handsome lawman at her side. Was it because Noah had returned fire? Or was the perpetrator attempting to get rid of anyone who would push to solve Brooke's murder? Felicity couldn't be sure, and it terrified her. Noah had a daughter who depended on him. Law enforcement was a dangerous job, yes, but this was different. They'd been targeted.

"Grady's being thorough." Noah reached inside the vehicle and broke open a case of water. He'd bought half a dozen while they were waiting, presumably for the homeless camp. He handed her a bottle. "Here. Drink this while I scrounge up some candy."

She sat up straighter. "What kind of candy?"

He dug around inside a go-bag and unearthed a packet of Twizzlers. The red kind. Her favorite. Felicity grinned as she snatched them out of Noah's hand. "Okay, this day just got a little better."

She ripped open the bag, tore off two strands of the roped licorice, and offered one to Noah. He accepted it with a wink that sent her heart rate skittering. Felicity mentally admonished herself as a flush crept across her cheeks. She wasn't some school girl with a crush. They'd just been shot at, for crying out loud.

Except... except something had transpired between her and Noah right before the shooting. For a moment, Felicity thought he was going to kiss her. Then again, it could've been her imagination running away with itself. Noah cared for her. Of that, she had no doubts. But that didn't mean he was interested in a romance. She needed to keep her focus on the case.

Tapping on her phone screen, she studied Jeremy

Lara's latest arrest photo while eating her candy. The man staring back at her appeared bewildered. His thinning hair was stuck out at all angles, his face gaunt with deep wrinkles running through the skin. He could've been anywhere from fifty to eighty, although his ID stated Jeremy was sixty-one. He'd been picked up by the sheriff's department for trespassing. His record reflected Noah's earlier observations. None of Jeremy's crimes were violent, but there were several arrests for verbal assaults.

"I see nothing in Jeremy's history that shows he's capable of planning Brooke's murder or these attacks on me." She narrowed her gaze. "We came here directly after leaving the Fergusons. Did you notice if the shooter looked like a woman?"

Noah frowned. "Everything happened quickly, but based on the height of the individual, I'd say we're looking for a man." He shrugged. "I'm not sure that helps us though. If either Kurtis or Melanie are tangled up in Brooke's murder, they wouldn't risk coming after us themselves. They'd hire someone."

She nodded in agreement. "They could've alerted the hitmen to our location."

"Or we were followed. I didn't spot a tail, but it's possible I missed it."

"Nope. I was watching for one too. There's no way both of us were fooled." She ripped off another rope of licorice just as Grady broke away from the witness and headed in their direction. Felicity jutted her chin toward her colleague. "Here we go."

Noah reached inside the vehicle and grabbed a water. He tossed it toward the Texas Ranger, who caught it with one hand. Grady twisted off the cap and drained the bottle in one go. He swiped at his mouth. "Thanks. This heat is brutal." He eyed Felicity's candy, and she handed him a strand. He bit off a chunk. "None of the witnesses could give a better description of the perpetrator than you did. Surveillance video caught the entire exchange. We were able to pull the license plate from that, but a police officer just reported to me that the truck was found abandoned in a grocery store parking lot about two miles from here."

"Who does the vehicle belong to?" Felicity took a long sip of her own water.

"Mr. Jessie Lyons. He was carjacked about thirty miles from here, outside a feed store, by a masked man. No witnesses. No video surveillance." Grady made a sour face. "Apparently, Mr. Lyons keeps a concealed handgun in his glove box. A Glock. It could be the weapon the perpetrator used to shoot at y'all today."

Her mind quickly put the pieces they had together. "The truck was stolen shortly after I arrived in town, indicating this man was the same individual who assaulted me at Brooke's house."

Noah nodded. "Witnesses reported seeing a silver truck speeding away after the fire, so I agree. It's probably the same guy." He turned to Grady. "Any chance a search of the truck yielded the weapon?"

"Afraid not. The truck is being towed to the forensic shed as we speak. Technicians will go over it with a fine-tooth comb. I'll keep you updated on what we find." He lifted off his cowboy hat and wiped at his forehead with the back of his sleeve. "Y'all are free to go. Thanks for hanging around in case I had additional questions."

Felicity handed him the rest of the Twizzlers. "Share these with the other officers, would you?"

"Sure thing." Grady's mouth thinned. "Be careful, Felicity. Whoever this guy is, he's determined. Shooting at two cops in broad daylight takes nerve."

She nodded, praying the technicians would find a lone fingerprint in the truck. Identifying the perpetrator would go a long way. In the meantime, she'd keep working Brooke's case. It was the fastest way to get to the bottom of things.

With a last wave to Grady, Felicity hopped into Noah's vehicle. The air-conditioning was a blessing after baking in the afternoon heat. She melted against the seat, letting the cool air wash over her face.

There was a conversation that needed to happen between her and Noah. One her conscience wouldn't let her avoid now that they were shielded from the prying eyes of everyone in the gas station parking lot.

She cleared her throat. "The shooter aimed for you. Maybe it was because you were returning fire, but it could've been because you're helping me investigate Brooke's case." Felicity hated the idea that her actions had placed him at risk. "You nearly died today. And yesterday. We have dangerous jobs, I get that, but this is turning out to be riskier than anyone could've antici-pated. Noah, you have a daughter. I wouldn't blame you one bit for passing this case over to the Rangers to handle."

He was quiet for a long moment, staring at the lake and the picnic table they'd eaten lunch at earlier. "I took an oath to protect this town. I refuse to let a pair of thugs threaten it. Or you." Noah's gaze swung to meet hers. The determination shimmering in the depths of his blue eyes was breathtaking. "I appreciate the consideration, Felicity, but I'm in this with you. Together, we're going to find the truth. You have my word."

ELEVEN

Noah's muscles were tense, and he was sporting the beginning of a headache when he turned onto the dirt road leading to the homeless camp. Afternoon sunlight glinted off the hood of the Tahoe. The inside of the cab smelled like french fries and warm burgers. Thanks to the shooting at the gas station, he'd chucked the meals purchased at the fast-food place—the summer heat had ruined them—but the bottles of water and the toiletries were fine.

Felicity gripped the handle over the door and peered through the windshield. "This place is pretty remote."

"Most of the residents prefer it. Out here, no one bothers them. The property belongs to the Jameson family. It's tied up in probate court, and while technically the tenants are trespassing, no one has demanded they be removed."

Ahead, a clearing appeared. Tents dotted the landscape, some disappearing into the trees. A common firepit was available to cook food or warm up if the night was chilly. Several beat-up vehicles sat under the shade created by thick pine branches.

Rick Paulson, unofficial leader, leaned against a makeshift table. His tennis shoes and T-shirt had holes and his jeans were muddy. A thick beard covered the lower half of his face. He squinted suspiciously until his gaze registered Noah at the wheel and then his expression softened.

"Let me do most of the talking." Noah cast a warning glance toward Felicity. "And stick close. These people don't take kindly to strangers."

She arched a brow. "Sounds like I should be worried."

"Naw. You're physically safe, but rub them the wrong way, and everyone in camp will clam up. They protect each other."

"Got it."

They exited the vehicle. Rick ambled over as Noah lifted the rear hatch. He eyed the supplies in the back of the Tahoe before turning a judgmental gaze on Felicity. "Who's that?"

"Ranger Capshaw. She's with me." Noah pulled out a bag of supplies and handed it to the older man before grabbing several cases of water. "You want these in the usual spot?"

"Yep." Rick spit a wad of tobacco juice toward a crop of nearby weeds. He took another bag from Felicity's outstretched hand so she could grab bottles of Gatorade.

"'Preciate the water. Heat wave a'coming and the stream is getting low. By August, we're gonna have to move someplace else if this keeps up."

Noah hauled the water onto the rickety table. The wood groaned in protest under the weight. The back of his neck itched with the feel of eyes on him, but he ignored the sensation. Most of the residents liked to steer clear of law enforcement. Some of them were addicts who'd had run-ins with the police and would again in the future. Others were simply leery. Once Noah and Felicity left, the people hiding in their tents would emerge to take advantage of the supplies.

Rick, for all his rudeness to strangers, was a fair leader. He doled out donations equally and never kept more for himself. Drug and alcohol abuse was tolerated in the camp, but not violence. Any theft resulted in immediate expulsion. Noah often wondered why Rick pursued this way of life. He'd asked him once, but the man had simply said that he liked being free to do as he pleased.

Noah glanced at the small riverbank several yards away. Sure enough, the water level was low. The camp used it for drinking, washing their clothes, and bathing. He envisioned heat stroke and death if the group didn't have enough access to fluids for hydration. "I'll let Pastor Isaiah at the church know. He'll organize a donation drive for y'all."

Rick spat another wad of tobacco juice in the weeds. "Don't bother. That man comes out here and preaches at us. We don't like it. Don't need none of that Jesus business."

In Noah's opinion, everyone could use more of that Jesus business, but he kept that thought to himself. "Easier to have a conversation or two with the pastor in exchange for water than packing up the entire camp."

The older man grunted, lifting a filthy ball cap from his head. Three strands of gray hair clung to his scalp. "I'll think about it." He settled the hat back in place and then squinted at Noah before jerking his chin toward Felicity. "Is she another do-gooder? Or is someone here in trouble with the law?"

"No one is in trouble, but we'd like to speak to Jeremy."

Rick's gaze narrowed. "If all you want to do is talk, then why bring her?"

Noah ignored the way the man refused to speak to or use Felicity's name. Yes, Rick was being purposefully rude, but calling it out would be counterproductive. "Ranger Capshaw is partnering with me on a case. Again, Jeremy isn't in trouble. We just need to ask him a few questions." He held Rick's gaze. "I've never lied to you before and have no reason to start now."

Rick mulled that over and then spat more tobacco juice. "Jeremy's in his usual spot, but he ain't doing so great." He pointed to his temple. "Ain't been right in the head for a couple of days. Tried to get him to eat yesterday, but he refused."

"Mind if I take him a few bottles of water?"

"Nope." He rummaged around inside a sack and

removed some beef jerky and a package of crackers. Rick tossed them to Noah. "Take those too. Maybe he'll eat something."

With a tilt of his head to indicate Felicity should follow, Noah shifted to a worn path weaving through the trees. He'd visited Jeremy enough times over the years to know where his regular campsite was. He kept his voice pitched low as the woods swallowed them up. "If Rick is right, and Jeremy is having a paranoid episode, then we probably won't get much from him. This may have been a wasted trip."

"That's okay. It's worth a go." She waved a fly away from her face. "Do you visit him often? Jeremy, I mean."

"From time to time." Noah ducked under a low-hanging branch. "One of the first call outs I responded to after joining the Knoxville PD was an attack on a woman in the homeless camp. While talking with her, a suspect came out of the woods and attacked me with a tire iron. Jeremy jumped into the fray with no concern for himself. His involvement is probably the only reason I'm here today."

He didn't want to think about the possibility that Jeremy, years earlier, had killed Brooke. Kurtis's statement had been suspect. Like Felicity, Noah didn't trust the man one iota, but he couldn't allow his feelings to cloud his judgment. He had to follow the evidence. No matter where it led. "I've tried several times to convince Jeremy to get into rehab, but he refuses. I pray for him all the time though. One day, I hope he'll accept help."

Felicity was quiet for a long moment. "In case I haven't said it lately, you're a good man, Noah Hodge."

Her words sent a warmth shooting straight through him. Noah was tempted to reach for her hand, but resisted. They were wading into dangerous territory, and now was not the time to let his heart rule his head. Instead, he gripped the bag of supplies tighter. "Just for the record, Fee, I think you're amazing too."

They continued in silence. The path grew slimmer as the woods became thicker. Overgrowth threatened to trip Noah. Sweat dripped down his back and a mosquito buzzed his ear. He held a low hanging branch away from the path and waited for Felicity to pass. Her cheeks were flush from exertion, but had no trouble keeping up with his rapid pace.

A few moments later, they reached a small campsite. Ancient pots covered in dirt hung from various branches. Rocks were arranged in strange patterns and various piles. Trash had been tied to the trees using different colored twine. A tent with a sagging middle was nestled against the shade of an oak tree. The firepit was nothing more than a hole in the ground crusted over with pine needles and leaves. It hadn't been used in a while. The whisper of a breeze skittered through the space and leaves rustled overhead. Birds sang.

Felicity planted her hands on her hips and turned in a circle. "Doesn't look like Jeremy is here."

Noah tilted his head toward the tent opening. Inside was a bundled sleeping bag. No sign of Jeremy. He raised his head and listened for any sound of human life. Bushes moved in the shadows. "Jeremy? It's Noah Hodge." He removed a bottle of water and waved it for the other man to see. "I've got some things for you. It's safe to come out."

The bushes moved again, and then a man emerged into the small clearing. Jeremy's hair flowed long over his shoulders. A beard covered the bottom half of his face. Deep lines marred the skin around his eyes and along his forehead, making him appear ancient. He was barefoot. Pants hung from his narrow hips and his shirt had long tears. Every inch of visible skin was dirty.

Noah kept his expression impassive as a wave of body odor mixed with sweat drifted on the breeze. He held out the bottle of water. "We brought food too."

Jeremy came up close, baring rotten teeth. He snatched the water bottle before drifting toward his tent. "They're coming. Danger. We must be ready." He spun toward Noah. "I'm building a bomb to protect us." He scurried over to a collection of metal objects. Spoons tangled together with broken wires and thread. "Soon it'll be ready."

Yep. Definitely in a paranoid state. Noah ignored Jeremy's comments, instead focusing on the task at hand. "I need to ask you some questions about Brooke Patterson."

Jeremy removed the cap from the water and drank deeply before adding some liquid to his "bomb" and muttering something under his breath. Then he flung the water bottle aside. He tugged on his long hair. "I need more time. A bit more time before we can be safe."

Felicity stepped around Noah. "Safe from who?"

Jeremy glanced up as if surprised by her voice. He blinked. Recognition sparked in the man's eyes before he rushed toward her. Noah stepped between them, but faster than he would've thought possible, Jeremy moved around him. The homeless man grabbed Felicity's arms. "You need to run! Go! Before the killer finds you."

Her mouth dropped open. Felicity reared back as if Jeremy had hit her. Her feet slipped on the pine needles and she tumbled to the ground, taking Jeremy with her. Noah rushed to their aid. He attempted to pry Jeremy's hands off Felicity, but the other man's grip was strong. "Let go of her!"

Felicity gaped like a fish out of water. She was stiff as a board, her gaze some place far away. Noah feared she was having some kind of panic attack. He was desperate to separate them, but didn't want to hurt either in the process.

Jeremy shook Felicity again. "Go! Run!"

As suddenly as Jeremy had grabbed Felicity, he released her. A second later, he was across the clearing and began rummaging through a duffel bag. The words he muttered were indecipherable.

Noah crouched next to Felicity and lightly touched her arm. "Breathe."

She blinked and then sucked in a breath. Then another. Felicity slowly turned her gaze toward him and the confusion cleared from her expression. It was replaced by shock. "Noah, he was there."

"What? Where?"

She trembled. "At Brooke's house. The night of the murder, Jeremy was there."

Leaves rustled on the ground and Noah turned. Jeremy approached with a balled-up shirt in his hands. The fabric was falling apart and dirty, but there was no mistaking the dark brown stains streaking across the light-blue fabric.

Blood.

TWELVE

Dusk painted the sky with brilliant shades of orange and lavender. Felicity drew in a deep breath of air scented with grass and earth. The heat of the day was finally cooling. A sweet summer breeze ruffled the strands of her hair and swept across her bare skin. She'd abandoned her cowboy hat in Noah's vehicle and undid the loose ponytail at the nape. The knots riding her shoulders streaked pain up her neck and into her temples. It'd been a long day. And it wasn't over yet.

"Are you sure about this?" Noah's voice rumbled across the distance between them. He stood at the front of his vehicle, broad shouldered and handsome as ever. Unlike her, there wasn't a hint of exhaustion in his expression or posture. "Aunt Imogene will understand if you need to take a raincheck on dinner."

Her gaze drifted to the farmhouse. It was picture perfect. A white clapboard with a wide front porch built for rocking chairs and sweet tea. Plants in hanging baskets dangled from the overhang. Roses arched up the trellis. A small slide and ball rested next to a covered sandbox. In the distance, horses grazed near a barn with a Texas flag painted on the side.

Some of Felicity's wariness eased as the thought of a home-cooked meal and happy conversation teased a smile from her lips. "No. I could use a break, and there's no way I'm turning down Imogene's famous fried chicken."

Noah's gaze studied her face for a heartbeat. Concern rode the strong line of his brow. She couldn't blame him. The incident with Jeremy had been intense. It'd taken over an hour to stop the trembling in her fingers. Even now, the lingering effects of the flashback threatened to unmoor her emotions.

He'd been there. Jeremy. With her in the house on the night of Brooke's murder. His touch and words had caused a flashback so vibrant, it'd catapulted Felicity back fifteen years. His warning had sent her running back upstairs and into the closet. Had the homeless man murdered her? Or, like Felicity, was he an eyewitness?

It was impossible to know. Noah had taken Jeremy's shirt into evidence and sent it straight to the crime lab. It would take a few days to determine if the blood on the fabric was a match for Brooke. A search of Jeremy's belongings yielded nothing else connected to the crime. Questioning him had gone nowhere. Ultimately, there was nothing more to do at the moment.

Waiting. Sometimes it was the worst part of the job.

"Daddy!"

The screen door flew open as Imogene appeared on

the porch, followed quickly by a toddler and a black Lab. The dog bounded down the steps and raced straight for Noah. He greeted the pup with several pats to the head before introducing him to Felicity. "This is Milo, the newest addition to our family."

Not to be outmaneuvered by the dog, Harper grasped Imogene's fingers and quickly scampered to even ground. Then, with a burst of energy, bolted straight for her father. "Daddy!" Harper's curls bounced with the force of her gait, and an infectious grin created dimples in her cheeks. She was dressed in shorts and a colorful top. Her feet were bare.

Noah bent over and caught his daughter in his arms, lifting her above his head in a move that caused a cascade of giggles. Harper wrapped herself around him like a spider monkey. The obvious love and affection between the two caused a lump in Felicity's throat. It'd been a year since her father passed away, but there were moments, just like this one, when she was reminded of how precious their relationship had been.

To make matters more complicated, a powerful yearning nearly stole Felicity's breath. This. This is what she wanted. A home with a man who adored his family and did everything he could for them. Her future wasn't with Noah—Felicity acknowledged his heart still belonged to Sally—but there was no harm in using him as an example of what could be.

Milo bounced over to Felicity and licked her hand in greeting. She showered the dog with affection. Then

Imogene shoed the animal away and enveloped Felicity in a warm hug.

"I'm so happy to see you." Imogene pulled back but held on to Felicity's arms. "Let me get a good look at you." Her astute gaze swept from Felicity's boot-clad feet to the top of her head. Imogene nodded knowingly. "Just as beautiful as ever, but you look tired and hungry. Two things I can help with."

She wrapped an arm around Felicity's waist and began guiding her up the porch steps. Harper's giggles trailed behind them as Noah gave the little girl a piggy-back ride through the yard. Milo followed, barking enthu-siastically.

Their joy eased the last of the tension from Felicity's muscles. She paused long enough to remove her shoes in the entryway and then followed Imogene into the sunny kitchen. A teenager with streaks of blue in her dark hair stood at the counter chopping tomatoes for a salad. Felicity greeted her with a wide smile. "Hey, Amber. How are you?"

Amber grinned back. "Fine, thanks."

"She's more than fine. Amber made the Honor Roll in the last semester of her junior year and has been tutoring other teens at the local youth center." Imogene beamed. "We're real proud of her."

Amber blushed at the compliment, but Felicity could tell she was absorbing Imogene's words like a flower takes in sunlight. It was amazing how love and attention could change a child's life. While living on the ranch, Amber had gone from being a constant runaway to a happy teen.

She wiped her hands on a dish towel and shrugged. "I didn't do anything special."

"It sounds pretty special to me. I'm impressed, Amber." Felicity glanced at the pile of plates and silverware resting on the counter. "Give me one minute to wash my hands and I'll be back to set the table."

"Nonsense!" Imogene planted her hands on her hips. "You're our guest."

Felicity wagged a finger as she moved toward the half-bath next to the pantry. "You can either let me set the table or I'll do the dishes afterward. Either way, I'm helping." Two minutes later, with clean hands and slightly tamed-down hair, she re-entered the kitchen and grabbed the plates. Easy conversation followed as Felicity caught up on the family happenings. The warm scents of freshly baked bread and fried chicken made her stomach growl.

The screen door opened and then slammed shut. Milo, followed by Harper, burst into the kitchen. The little girl ran straight for Imogene and hid behind her legs. Childish laughter gave away her poor hiding spot, as did the black Lab, who was busy licking her bare arm. Felicity watched with amusement as Noah entered the room. His hair was mussed from playing in the yard and grass blades clung to the bottom of his pants.

"Where's Harper?" He faked looking around the room, including under the table. Noah ruffled Amber's hair in greeting as he squeezed past her to open the pantry. "Harper! We have to wash our hands for dinner."

The little girl giggled some more. Her laugh was

infectious and soon everyone was chuckling. Felicity knew without being told that this game was a frequent one in the household. The juxtaposition between the horrible day and this warm moment wasn't lost on her. On the drive over, Noah explained he did everything possible to have dinner with his family and be the one to put his daughter to bed. She understood why. These moments of joy were important.

Noah "found" Harper with a roar and swept her over his shoulder, carting her off to the bathroom. Several minutes later, they returned. He sat down at the table next to Felicity, holding his daughter in his lap.

Harper suddenly seemed to register Felicity's presence because she clapped her hands. "Fee!"

"Hi." Felicity smiled back. She reached into her purse and pulled out a pop-up book she'd purchased at the gas station. There was also candy in her bag, but she'd save that for after dinner. "This is for you."

The little girl's eyes glowed with happiness as she took the book. Noah bounced his legs to grab Harper's attention. "What do you say?"

"Thank you."

The sweet gratitude sent an ocean of tenderness surging through Felicity. "You're welcome, sweetie. I like your T-shirt." She pointed to the strawberry dancing across the fabric. "Do you know what color that is?"

"Red!" Harper shouted the word and then bounced on her dad's legs. "Red strawberry."

Imogene placed a bowl of green beans on the table.

"Harper knows most of her colors, but since strawberries are her favorite fruit, she remembers red very well."

"She's a smart girl." Felicity wiggled her fingers and moved them closer, as if she was going to tickle Harper. The little one squealed with excitement. She resembled Sally so much, from the curly hair down to the bow-shaped mouth. Even her laugh resonated with the echo of her late mother's lilting voice. "Strawberries are my favorite fruit too."

Noah kissed the top of Harper's head before placing her in the highchair next to him. He strapped her in securely before retaking his seat. "Aunt Imogene, this smells delicious. Let's all sit and say grace. I'm starving."

Imogene and Amber joined them at the table. Noah took one of Harper's chubby hands gently in his own before offering his other hand to Felicity. She hesitated and then slipped her fingers across his palm. The moment their skin touched, a jolt of electricity coursed through her. Noah's touch was warm and familiar but incredibly different at the same time.

Their gazes met. A spark of something akin to attraction flared in Noah's eyes. Felicity's pulse kicked up a notch. It reminded her of the moments right before the shooting when she'd sensed he wanted to kiss her. Was she imagining his interest? Or was it genuinely there? And if so, what did that mean?

Noah gently squeezed her hand and then bowed his head. Felicity clasped hands with Amber, who was seated on her other side and then followed suit.

"Lord, we thank You for the food before us."

Imogene's voice was thick with emotion. "We thank You for gathering us all together to enjoy this dinner together and ask for Your continued protection, especially over Noah and Felicity. Guide them in their search for the truth. In Your name, we pray. Amen."

A chorus of amens followed. Then everyone passed plates of food, helping themselves to the wonderful feast that included fresh rolls and creamy mashed potatoes. The conversation flowed as they discussed everything from running the ranch to Amber's upcoming summer camp.

Finally, Felicity put the last bite of food in her mouth and leaned back in her chair. "I ate enough for three people. Imogene, you outdid yourself. Everything was amazing."

"Thank you, dear. Of course, I hope you saved room for dessert. We've got fresh brownies and vanilla ice cream."

"Ice cream." Harper wriggled in her highchair. "Me ice cream. Me. Harper ate well."

The plastic plate in front of her held remnants of her dinner. She'd eaten most of the food, save for a few green beans. Noah stabbed one with his fork and offered it to her. "One more bite and then ice cream."

The little girl dutifully opened her mouth. From the way her nose wrinkled after Noah fed her the green bean, the vegetable wasn't her favorite. Felicity smothered a laugh behind her hand. Making sure she kept her voice to a whisper, she leaned over and said, "I don't think she likes them."

He chuckled. "Agreed. She tolerates them because eating dinner is the only way to dessert." He kept his voice low enough the toddler couldn't overhear. "If Harper had her way, she'd live off ice cream and strawberries."

"Sounds reasonable to me."

Noah glowered. "Don't you dare tell her that."

Felicity laughed. Harper leaned over to see around her dad and grinned. Her dimples were adorable.

Noah's cell phone rang. He groaned and fished it out of his pocket. He glanced at the screen and then back at her. "It's Tucker." Noah answered the call, rising from the table, tossing an apologetic look toward his foster mother who was plating brownies. "Hodge."

Felicity followed him out of the kitchen and into a small office.

Noah listened for a few moments and then said, "Meet us at Felicity's rental house in an hour." He hung up and turned to her. His forehead was creased with confusion. "Technicians located a partial print on the dash on the passenger side of the abandoned truck. They ran it through the criminal databases and got a hit. We know who the shooter is."

She braced herself for bad news. "Who is it?"

THIRTEEN

Noah took a seat at the dining room table next to Felicity. The hearty dinner sat like a lump in the pit of his stomach as stress and worry tangled his insides. Across from him, Tucker's expression was grim. He wore his uniform, although it was wrinkled along the chest from a long shift and his jaw was shadowed with beard growth. Grady looked equally worn out. The Texas Ranger was still wearing the same clothing as earlier and the circles under his eyes were darker than before.

The scent of fresh coffee filled the tiny space. Everyone had a mug of the dark brew, along with one of Imogene's homemade brownies, which she'd packaged up for their meeting. Noah took a swig of his drink and instantly regretted it. The flavor was perfect, but his stomach couldn't handle the acidity. Beside him, Felicity twisted her mug but didn't drink from it. Worry lines bracketed her mouth. He wanted to reach across the distance between them and gather her into his arms. To hold her until the tension riding her shoulders disappeared.

In the last twenty-four hours, she'd been pushed down the stairs, nearly burned alive, and shot at. Felicity didn't deserve this. No one did. But the fact that it was her life in danger... it sparked a protective streak inside Noah that was fierce and undeniable.

He would do anything to protect her. *Anything.*

Noah was used to putting his life on the line for strangers. He was a cop, after all. But this was different. The risk was greater and becoming more so with every passing minute. The wisest thing would be to pass this case over to the Rangers. They would protect Felicity and make sure justice was done. Noah had a daughter to think about. A little girl who'd already lost her mother and needed her dad. Mentally, he knew what the logical answer was. But he couldn't do it. His heart wouldn't allow him to walk away from Felicity.

What did that mean? Noah wasn't sure. He cared for her, that much was certain, but these feelings were far more than mere friendship. He couldn't pinpoint when things had shifted between them. It was long after Sally's death, but before yesterday. It added another layer to an already confusing and tangled mess.

Noah pushed aside his coffee and focused on Grady and Tucker. "Okay, bring us up to speed."

Grady set a photograph on the dining room table. "The shooter is Gene Webb. Thirty-one. He has a rap sheet longer than my arm, going as far back as his teens.

Possession, theft, armed robbery, bombing, attempted murder. You name it, he's been involved in it."

Noah studied the mug shot. Gene's head was shaved. Tattoos crisscrossed the visible skin above the collar of his shirt and crept up his chin. His eyes were small and hard. Anger and hatred seemed to pour off him, vibrant enough to be captured in the photograph. The information listed under the mug shot described him as six feet and a bulky 230. From the curve of his shoulders, it appeared to be more muscle than fat.

He pushed the picture toward Felicity. "Does he look familiar?"

"No." She frowned. "I don't understand. What is Gene's connection to Brooke?"

"That's a good question, and it's not one we can answer yet. Gene is originally from this area, but as his arrest record reflects, has spent most of his time in Houston. Gene is linked to Triple 6."

Felicity reared back. "The organized crime ring?"

"Yep. Triple 6 traffics in drugs, guns, and people. Several departments—including the FBI and ATF—have tried to infiltrate the organization to shut them down but without success. No one knows who the leader of Triple 6 is. We've captured and convicted a few of the lower-level drug dealers, but they've refused to cooperate, even if it means a lighter prison sentence."

Noah's mind whirled with the information. "What connection does Gene have with Triple 6?"

"Informants have identified him as an enforcer. We've been unable to confirm that information though."

Grady turned to Felicity. "Is it possible Brooke was working for Triple 6?"

Felicity stiffened. "No way. Brooke wasn't a criminal, nor did she hang out with them. Nothing uncovered during the initial murder investigation shows she was into anything illegal."

Grady shrugged. "With all due respect, we can't rely on the initial investigation. I don't want to take the possibility off the table." He held up a finger. "However, there is another potential explanation. Brooke's killer could've hired Gene to silence you."

"Is there anything in Gene's history that indicates he'd been contracted to murder someone before?"

"An accusation from three years ago." Tucker flipped to a page in a copied report. "Houston Police Department couldn't verify the information, so Gene was never charged, but he allegedly murdered a plastic surgeon. Gunned him down in the parking lot of his office." His mouth hardened. "Happened in broad daylight. The killer used a stolen vehicle, which was recovered a few miles away in a store parking lot. He was never caught. The doctor's wife inherited millions and had a tenuous connection to Triple 6. It's suspected her dry-cleaning business is used as a front to launder money."

Noah's spine stiffened. "And HPD couldn't prove the wife had hired Gene?"

"There was no exchange of money or strange withdrawals from her bank accounts."

"Doesn't mean much. If she planned the murder, the wife could've easily pulled money out of the account over time and paid the killer in cash." Noah didn't like the similarities between the doctor's murder and the shooting at the gas station. "Killers are creatures of habit, just like the rest of us. If Gene murdered the doctor, then he's used a drive-by shooting style before."

Grady nodded. "It's something to consider. But why didn't Gene use an automatic weapon this afternoon? Surely he has access to them as a gang member. An AR-15 would've been a much better choice for a drive-by shooting."

"He didn't use one to kill the doctor." Tucker broke off a piece of brownie and popped it in his mouth. "A 9mm was used in the commission of that crime. If you look at his rap sheet, most of the violent crimes he's been arrested for involve a handgun. My guess: after his first attempt to kill Felicity failed, he used an older method that had worked for him in the past." His gaze met Noah's and his brows arched. "Like you said, a creature of habit."

"I assume you've put a BOLO out on Gene."

A BOLO was short for be-on-the-lookout. It meant every law enforcement officer in the state would be searching for the criminal.

Grady nodded. "We've also got officers knocking on the doors of his family members and known comrades." He drained the last of his coffee. "In the meantime, a trooper is stationed outside to keep watch over Felicity tonight. Hopefully, we'll have a solid lead on Gene's whereabouts in the morning."

Felicity rested her hands on the back of the chair.

"We have an appointment tomorrow morning with Melanie Ferguson. As Brooke's best friend, she'll have a deeper insight into what was going on in Brooke's life before the murder." She provided Grady and Tucker with a rundown of everything they knew so far. "If my flashback is right—and I believe it is—then Jeremy was in the house on the night of the murder. He likely witnessed it, but questioning him won't be effective while he's in a paranoid state. We'll know more once the shirt is analyzed by the lab."

Grady tilted his head. "Is it possible Jeremy murdered Brooke?"

"Initially I thought so, but I can't see Jeremy hiring Gene to kill me. He doesn't have the funds, for starters." Her forehead creased. "Jeremy told me to run on the night of Brooke's murder. I think he was trying to protect me." She hugged herself tighter. "Brooke told her brother she was dating someone new, but Daniel didn't know who. Neither did Kurtis. It's possible this mystery boyfriend is connected to Triple 6. Hopefully, talking to Melanie tomorrow morning will help fill in the gaps."

The men rose from the table, and after a few last words, Grady and Tucker left.

Felicity picked up their empty mugs and carried them to the sink. Her shoulders were tense and worry hung like a cloud in the small home decorated in soothing grays and browns.

Noah piled the rest of the plates together and took them into the kitchen. "You wash, I'll dry."

She tossed him a weak smile and filled the sink with

soapy water. Noah could practically hear the wheels in her head spinning. He picked up a dishtowel. "It might help if you share those thoughts running around inside your head. If you don't, I'm afraid your brain might overheat."

The comment earned him a laugh, as he hoped. Some of the tension eased from her shoulders. Noah took a dripping plate from her, waiting patiently. He'd learned a long time ago that sometimes she just needed a few minutes to gather her thoughts. He'd expressed support. Now it was up to her to accept the offer or not.

Felicity handed him another dish and used the back of her hand to swipe at a loose curl. "I'm mulling over the possibilities. Gene could've been hired by someone to kill me. Kurtis is a criminal court judge. Is it possible they crossed paths that way? Or am I reaching for an explanation because I dislike Kurtis?" She swiped aggressively at a coffee mug. "I can't stop thinking that he manipulated us today. Sent us searching for Jeremy, who had a blood-stained item that is probably going to come back linked to Brooke."

"How would Kurtis know that you'd remember Jeremy? Or that Jeremy still had that shirt?"

"He wouldn't." She blew out a breath and shook her head. "That's what I mean. My visceral dislike for Kurtis is clouding my logic. That argument he had with Brooke... I can't stop thinking about it. He was angry and verbally vicious, but people get mad. Couples argue. It doesn't make him a killer."

Noah prided himself on following the evidence, but

there was a place for gut instinct too. Felicity had witnessed Brooke's murder. Maybe her emotions were trying to communicate something her brain already knew. "Right now, Kurtis isn't at the top of our suspect list, but I didn't like the way he handled our interview today either. There's a guy at the police department who's fantastic at digging into people's backgrounds."

Detective Jax Taylor had been a top-notch research analyst for the FBI before coming home to take care of his aging parents. His skill set with the computer and financial data couldn't be matched. "I'll ask Jax to check for a connection between Kurtis and Gene." Noah reconsidered. "Actually, it might be a good idea to see if Brooke's brother and Gene know each other. Daniel was forthcoming during our interview, but he owns a handgun similar to the one used to murder Brooke. It's worth digging into a bit more."

Felicity handed him the last plate and then popped the drain so the water could run out. "Thank you."

"For what?" He folded the dish towel and set it on the counter.

"For... everything. This would be much harder to handle if you weren't with me."

The woman had a way of making him feel like a superhero. "Aww, Fee. Come here." Noah pulled her into his arms, her strawberry-scented shampoo teasing his senses as he kissed the top of her head. Felicity sighed, nestling her face in the crook where his neck met his shoulder. Her breath was warm against the exposed skin along his collar.

The embrace was supposed to be friendly, a way to comfort her, but Noah couldn't ignore the way she felt in his arms. It was... right. He absently rubbed the knots in the muscles along her neck. Her skin was silky smooth. Noah could've stood there all night holding her, but it was getting late and they both needed rest.

With regret, he released her. "I should go."

She walked him to the front door. Noah lingered in the entryway. He didn't like leaving her alone in the house all night, even with a trooper stationed at the end of the driveway. "Would you like me to sleep on the couch tonight? Or I could call Cassie? She and Nathan would come in a heartbeat."

Felicity's mouth turned up at the corners. "That's a kind offer, but no thank you. I can protect myself." She gestured toward the window. The outline of a trooper's vehicle parked on the street was visible through the gauze fabric. "And I've got backup. I'll be okay." Her hand landed on his chest. "Go home to your daughter, Noah."

He cupped her fingers with his own, stepping closer until they were mere inches apart. Giving in to his desire, Noah brushed a curl away from her forehead. Felicity inhaled sharply. Her gaze lifted to meet his. He trailed a finger across her cheek and down to her chin. "I'm a phone call away if you need me."

"I know."

She rose on her tiptoes and placed a kiss on his cheek. It was quick and spontaneous, but his heart rate spiked. He was tempted to capture her lips with his own, but that one move could put their entire friendship at risk. Noah hesitated. Felicity froze. Their gazes met. A mixture of emotions was buried in the depths of her beautiful brown eyes. Desire tangled with fear. In that instant, Noah realized that whatever attraction he was feeling, she shared it. These worries about screwing everything up were ones she had as well.

It'd been a long day. They'd nearly died twice. Once in the fire yesterday and then today at the gas station. It wasn't smart to kiss Felicity. There were a dozen reasons this would be a colossal disaster—starting with the fact that they were working a case together—but Noah didn't have the strength to resist any longer. To fight these feelings for her that'd formed over the last year and were growing with every breath. Especially not when Felicity was looking at him with so much yearning.

He leaned forward, brushing her lips with his. Testing. Hesitant. Giving her time to back away if she thought better of it. She didn't. He persisted with a series of featherlight kisses that sent his pulse racing and swallowed his senses so that all he knew was her.

Felicity's arms wound around his neck and he pulled her closer, finally deepening the kiss.

And just like that, he was lost.

FOURTEEN

The next morning, Felicity nursed a cup of coffee. Her eyes felt gritty and exhaustion weighed on her, but she couldn't imagine going back to bed. The case—and the kiss with Noah—had caused a restless night's sleep. She'd finally tossed the covers off at five. The first trail of sunshine drifted across the tile floor while she reviewed the case file.

Had Brooke been involved with Triple 6? It was hard to believe the kindhearted woman who'd cooked her pancakes for breakfast was part of a ruthless criminal organization, but Felicity had learned early on in her career that people were not always what they seemed.

She turned to a photo buried in the file. It was of Brooke and Kurtis. He had an arm slung around the young woman's shoulders in a possessive hold. The other hand held a beer. Brooke's smile was wide, but there were signs of strain around the edges and tension in her posture.

There was no date on the photograph, so there was no way of knowing when it'd been taken. There also weren't any notes about the item in the case file. Felicity had no idea why it was there, except... maybe the former chief didn't quite believe Kurtis was as innocent as he claimed.

Suspicions and questions. That's all Felicity had at the moment. She flipped to Gene Webb's mug shot. His stony stare iced her blood. It wasn't difficult to imagine him killing someone for money. Is that why he was hunting her? It was the most logical answer. Hopefully, Noah's colleague would uncover a connection between Gene and someone else on their suspect list.

God, help guide us to the right answer. Use me as Your instrument to get justice and stop a killer before—

A knock on the front door interrupted her prayer. Felicity's heart rate spiked as her head snapped up. Through the gauzy curtain covering the living room window, a shadow lingered on the porch. She slid up to the door, one hand on her weapon, and peeked out. Then breathed a sigh of relief. Cassie and Leah.

She swung the door open wide. The scent of warm cinnamon tangled with a blast of humid air. Cassie, her growing belly encased in a dress, smiled brightly. In one hand, she held a box of pastries. Leah hefted her daughter, Sophia, higher on her hip. The little girl wore shorts and a T-shirt. One hand was coated in drool and slimy crumbs as she gummed a cookie. At the end of the driveway, Tucker and Nathan were talking with the trooper guarding the house.

Felicity smiled at her friends, while raising a hand in greeting to the men. "Morning everyone. What a pleasant surprise."

"We brought breakfast." Leah stepped over the threshold. "Glad to see we didn't wake you."

"Nope. I've been up for a while." She hesitated, glancing back at the men who were busy digging into their own pastry box. The trooper set aside the coffee mug Felicity had taken out to him earlier and extracted a bear claw. "The guys aren't coming in?" Felicity arched her brows at Cassie. "They don't have to eat in the driveway."

She waved a hand dismissively. "They don't mind. Trust me, on deployment they ate in a lot worse places than your front yard."

Leah snorted. "Sometimes I think they prefer roughing it." She wriggled her brows. "Keeps them manly."

Felicity eyed her good friends as she shut the front door. "It also allows them to watch over the property while you guys are here."

Cassie nodded. "That too. Our husbands can be over-protective at times, but in this instance, I think they're right. You were nearly shot yesterday. I don't know about you, but having a few extra men guarding the property doesn't hurt." She threaded an arm through Felicity's and tugged her toward the kitchen. "What I can't understand is why you didn't call us last night? Nathan and the others would've provided protection without question."

It was a kind offer. Cassie and Leah's husbands were

part of a friendship circle known affectionately as the Special Forces to law enforcement. All former military, they provided protection to individuals in danger.

Felicity took the pastry box from her friend and set it on the table. "I had a trooper outside my door all night. Tucker is busy working the case." He was a part of the Special Forces but worked for the Knoxville PD and had duties to uphold. Felicity crossed to the coffee machine and poured Leah a cup. "And there was no need to bother Nathan."

"You aren't *bothering* anyone." Leah settled into a chair with Sophia. The sweet little girl gummed her biscuit and then pounded the hard end on the table as if to punctuate her mother's words. "We're your friends, Felicity, and you're in danger. We want to help. No disrespect to the trooper. I'm sure he's good at his job, but he's no match for five—six, including Tucker—former military men. If you use them, then Noah won't have to spend the night in his SUV keeping guard."

Her words stopped Felicity cold. "What?" She blinked. "Noah was here?"

"He left shortly before we arrived." Cassie's brows arched slightly as she took the glass of water Felicity offered. "You didn't know."

"No." Felicity closed her eyes. Some Texas Ranger she was. "I thought he'd gone home. It never occurred to me..." She sank into the chair, realizing her mistake. Of course, Noah wouldn't leave her. Not after the shooting. He'd been worried Gene would make a move while she was vulnerable and sleeping.

Cassie eyed her knowingly. "He cares about you. More than just as a friend and colleague. And unless I'm misjudging the way you two have been interacting over the last several months, you care about him too."

"It's complicated." Felicity absently touched her lips with a forefinger as the memory of last night's embrace replayed in her mind. Her stomach tightened. No one had ever made her feel like that before. Cherished and wanted and feminine. The intensity of her emotions shocked her. She'd known there was attraction and friendship, but the kiss they'd shared had revealed the true depth of her feelings for Noah. She was dangerously close to falling in love with the man. A terrifying proposition. Noah would never purposefully hurt her, but was he capable of truly moving on after losing his wife?

More importantly, was she ready to date a single dad? To step into the role of caregiver to a little girl who'd already lost so much? Compromise would be required. Her career wouldn't be front and center anymore. Felicity didn't want to spend her life alone, but facing the reality of making different choices was unsettling. Was she truly capable of doing this?

Her dad hadn't been. Michael Capshaw had been a loving man who cared deeply for his daughter, but his career had always taken priority. He'd missed holidays, birthdays, and school plays. A part of Felicity had resented her dad. As an adult, that pain softened with understanding. He'd worked hard to put food on the table, but more importantly, his job as an emergency room physician saved lives. Michael took that seriously. Had instilled that same work ethic into his daughter.

It'd been foolish to kiss Noah. She'd been caught up in the moment, but the cold light of morning brought a sense of clarity. They were working a case. The last thing either of them needed was to rock the boat and make working together awkward. Unfortunately, Felicity feared that was exactly what'd happened.

Cassie opened the bakery box, revealing an array of freshly baked pastries. "Most relationships are complicated. Nathan and I had a rocky start." She handed Felicity a blueberry scone. "Leah and Tucker were nearly killed by a psychopath before figuring out they loved each other."

"Yep. Plus Tucker was unemployed and struggling with his faith in God when we met." Leah bounced Sophia on her knee. "The road to happiness isn't always easy, but don't forget that you have people here who love and care about you, Felicity. I don't think I'm speaking out of turn when I include Noah in that statement."

"I know." Felicity broke off a piece of her scone. "And I won't deny things have shifted in our relationship lately, but Noah's heart was broken when his wife died. I'm not sure he's ready to move on to something new. And I..." She frowned. "As much as I want a family, I don't know if I'm capable of putting my career second."

Why was she even talking about this? It'd been one kiss. One kiss.

One steamy, over-the-moon kiss.

Her cheeks flushed, but Felicity mentally admonished herself. One kiss didn't mean Noah wanted a relationship. Things were heightened, emotions were running amuck. He might have regretted it the moment he stepped out of her house last night.

And yet something deep inside Felicity told her the kiss meant something. Noah Hodge wasn't the kind of man who gave into his desires easily. He'd probably been thinking about her for as long as she'd been thinking about him. Her heart pattered a bit faster at the realization.

"Have you talked to Noah about your concerns?" Cassie asked. "Or about how much you care for him?"

"No, but I'm sure after last night, he has some idea about how I feel." The heat in her cheeks increased. "We kissed." She groaned and pushed her scone away. "I've got a killer hunting me. Brooke's case is complicated and getting more so with every piece of evidence we uncover. Is it possible to develop deep and powerful feelings for someone when everything is in chaos?"

Cassie and Leah shared a look. They both grinned and said in unison, "Yes."

Felicity laughed lightly. She should've anticipated their answer. "So what do I do now?"

FIFTEEN

Knoxville Bank was located off Main Street, across from a pet store and next door to an ice cream shop. Traffic in town was heavier than normal, and Noah had to circle the block twice before finding a free parking spot at the end of the street. Signs boasted summer sales in the store windows. Despite the heat, residents were out and about. A group of teens, dressed for the pool in flip-flops and coverups, laughed as they crossed the street, heading for a fast-food joint in search of snacks.

Everything appeared normal. Still, Noah wouldn't let his guard down for a moment. Not until Gene was in police custody. His gaze scanned the street once more before he allowed his muscles to relax. He tilted his face toward the sunshine, soaking in a bit of Vitamin D, in the hopes it would erase the last of his fatigue. After keeping watch on Felicity's house for most of the night, he'd gone home to kiss his daughter good morning and catch a precious few hours of sleep. A strong dose of caffeine and a hearty meal from Aunt Imogene had gone a long way to bolstering his mood. So did being with Felicity.

"I hope you're wearing sunscreen, cowboy." She joined him on the sidewalk. Her hair was tucked into a low ponytail, her eyes cast in shadows under the brim of her hat. Felicity's mouth twitched playfully. "It's gonna be awfully hard to woo the single ladies around here if you're wrinkly from too much sun exposure."

He briefly touched the dent in her chin. "There's only one lady I'm interested in wooing."

The words flowed naturally. Last night's kiss had opened the door to a new aspect of their relationship. Flirtation. Noah realized he'd been walking on eggshells around Felicity for months, desperately watching every word, fearful she'd uncover his hidden feelings. He didn't have to do that anymore. It was a relief.

A pretty flush appeared on her cheeks, and Felicity's smile widened. Noah's heart skipped several beats. He grinned back. They hadn't discussed the kiss or what it meant yet. Noah wasn't ignorant about the issues facing a long-term relationship with Felicity. For starters, there was his daughter to consider. She needed his time and emotional energy. Then there was his job. It was demanding and often required long hours. Felicity's did too. Both of them faced potential danger every time they went to work. Noah had already been through the death of his parents and his wife. The thought of losing someone else he cared about... it was enough to stall his breath and send his heart searching for the nearest exit off the freeway of emotional entanglement.

All of it was too much to sort out at the moment. Kissing Felicity last night hadn't been the wisest course of action since they still had to work together. He didn't regret it though. Nor did he know where it was leading. All he knew was that thinking too much allowed fear to grab hold, and *that* had been an issue in their relationship for far too long. For them both.

Noah's phone rang, pulling his attention away from Felicity's gorgeous smile. He removed it from his pocket and glanced at the screen. "It's Jax. I asked him to look for any connection between Kurtis and Gene first thing this morning." He answered, stepping into the shade of an awning. "What ya got?"

"A big fat nothing." Jax's Southern drawl poured from the phone speaker. "Gene has never appeared in Kurtis's court, nor can I find any connection between the two men. Kurtis has overseen cases involving the Triple 6 organization but hasn't given them leniency. In fact, the exact opposite. He's ordered the maximum sentencing for most of the offenders."

"Okay, that probably means he's not the leader of Triple 6 or connected to them."

"Agreed. I also did a cursory glance at Melanie, to make sure she wasn't connected to Gene, and came up empty-handed. I'll look a bit more, but so far, the couple is squeaky clean."

"Understood. Thanks."

Noah hung up and relayed the information to Felicity.

She took the news with a stoic nod. "Based on what

we know so far, I think we need to drop Kurtis and Melanie down on our suspect list. They alibied each other for the night of Brooke's murder and we can't connect them to Gene." Her gaze drifted to the bank. "I think we need to use Melanie as a resource. Let's question her about Gene, Brooke's brother, Daniel, and her mysterious new boyfriend."

"Sounds like a plan."

Noah fell into step beside Felicity, and moments later, they were escorted by a bank employee to Melanie Ferguson's office overlooking the busy street. Large windows spilled sunshine across the plush carpet and mahogany desk. Enclosed bookcases lined one wall. The other held photographs of Melanie alongside several influential members of the state. Noah recognized the governor and a senator.

Melanie rose from her leather desk chair and greeted them each with a handshake. Today she wore a silk dress under a blazer that perfectly matched the rosy color of her painted lips. A blast of air-conditioning hit Noah on the back of his neck when he settled into the wingback chair across from Melanie's desk. "Thank you for taking the time to meet with us, Mrs. Ferguson."

"Of course. Brooke's death was so... shocking." She reclaimed her seat behind the desk. "Were you able to speak to Jeremy? Kurtis explained he'd shared his concerns about the repairman to you yesterday."

Noah wasn't surprised that Kurtis and Melanie had discussed the case. They were married, and Brooke had been close to both of them. "We did, ma'am. Kurtis was helpful during our interview and we're following up on all leads." He removed a photograph of Gene Webb from the front pocket of his suit jacket and laid it on the desk. "Have you seen this man before?"

Melanie pulled the picture closer. Her expression was difficult to read, but no flash of recognition flickered across her features. She shook her head. "No. Who is he?"

"Someone we believe is connected to Brooke's murder." Noah tilted his head, studying the woman's expression carefully. "We believe he's connected to a criminal organization known as Triple 6. Have you ever heard of it?"

"In the news." She shook her head, hair shimmering in the sun. "But I don't understand what this has to do with Brooke."

"We're not sure either." Felicity leaned forward. "Triple 6 is a shadowy criminal enterprise known for selling drugs and illegal guns. They operate throughout this area, as well as Houston and Dallas. Brooke may have crossed paths with someone from Triple 6. Can you think of anything that was going on in her life that would connect her to either Triple 6 or this man?" She pointed to the photograph of Gene.

Melanie stared at her for a long moment before pushing away from her desk. She rose on pinprick heels and went to the window, wrapped her arms around her midsection. Noah shared a glance with Felicity. Clearly, Melanie was struggling with the need to share some piece of information. The silence stretched out. Noah let it.

Sometimes, it was better to let the witness lead the conversation.

Finally she turned to face them. "Daniel, Brooke's brother, was trafficking drugs for several years. I don't know if he was working for Triple 6 specifically, but if what you're saying is true, and they operate in this area, then it's possible."

Noah's muscles stiffened slightly, but he kept his tone professional. "How do you know Daniel was trafficking drugs?"

"Because Brooke uncovered paraphernalia in the shed at the rear of her property. She freaked out, threatened to turn her brother in. Daniel swore up and down that he'd only used her place as a temporary holding space because the police had recently arrested him on possession charges. He was on probation and worried they'd search his place. Daniel promised to keep her out of it. Brooke relented."

"When did this happen?"

"About two months before her death." Melanie chewed on her lip as tears filmed her eyes. "I didn't tell the police at the time because Daniel was so distraught over Brooke's death. He's struggled with drug use for a long time and was having a lot of financial problems, which is how he got roped into trafficking. Considering he was using her shed as a backup hiding place, it made little sense for him to kill her."

Not unless Brooke threatened to go to the police again. Daniel had several arrests for minor drug possession, but trafficking was a felony. A conviction would mean serious jail time. Noah chewed that over. "If Brooke found out Daniel had broken his promise and used the shed again, would she have turned him into the police?"

Melanie shrugged. "I don't know. Brooke was smart, but she had a soft spot for her brother." She removed a tissue from a box on the credenza and dabbed at her eyes. "I should've pushed her to go to the police from the beginning. Then maybe…"

She'd still be alive. Regret was a painful pill to swallow, and while Noah had sympathy for Melanie, he was also angry that she'd hid a vital piece of information about Brooke from law enforcement for so long. From the tightness bracketing Felicity's mouth, she shared his feelings.

Sunshine winking off glass caught Noah's attention. What on earth was that? It disappeared and then came back behind an oversized truck parked on the street. His heart skittered as the realization of what he was seeing slammed into him with the force of a sledgehammer. Instinctively, his body rose to a crouch, ready to spring toward Felicity, even as a warning flew from his lips.

"Sniper!"

SIXTEEN

Felicity hit the carpet with a bone-jarring crash as bullets from a semiautomatic rifle slammed into the window. Noah covered her with his body in a protective embrace. Shattering glass and screams filled the bank. The noise was deafening and sent her heart into overdrive. Adrenaline shot through her system. Time slowed down. She was achingly aware of the roar of her pulse, the feel of Noah's skin against her own, and the rapid beat of steady shots raining down on them. Silent prayers winged through her heart.

An explosion vibrated the earth. More screams followed. Smoke and dust hazed the air. Felicity grabbed hold of Noah's hand covering her head and held on. His strong and capable fingers gripped hers. The world was falling apart around them, and Felicity would never wish harm on anyone, especially Noah, but she was eternally grateful for his presence. His protection.

Trust in God. Let your heart lead you.

Cassie's advice earlier this morning at the breakfast table rippled through Felicity's mind. She wasn't very good at surrendering, especially in romance, but as chaos reigned, she understood the words of wisdom in a new way. She had to place her trust in Him in all ways. In this moment. In her relationship with Noah. In her doubts about herself.

Lord, I surrender. I'm so scared. Please help me get through this moment with Noah. Protect the innocent lives in danger. Guide my thoughts so I can remember what happened to Brooke.

The petition centered the whirlwind of her thoughts. Felicity realized the shots had stopped, and the screams had lessened to whimpers. She squeezed Noah's hand before lifting her head.

Melanie's office was torn apart. The window was demolished by the gunfire. Papers littered the carpet and smoke drifted through the sunshine like a strange fog. Felicity's lungs burned with the faint hint of an indistinguishable chemical. She sucked in a shallow breath. "Noah, you okay?"

"I'm okay." He shifted to his knees and pulled his weapon. "Stay down. I'll check for the sniper."

They'd been sheltered from most of the gunshots by Melanie's huge desk. Felicity pulled her own weapon and belly-crawled to the opposite edge. Where was Melanie? Had she been hit? The smoke stung her eyes, and she blinked against the tears forming along her lashes. "Melanie!"

A moan reached Felicity's ears. She peeked around

the desk and her heart dropped to her stomach before launching back into her throat. Melanie rested against the bookcases in a small alcove of protection. She clutched her side. Blood was rapidly spreading like a stain across her silk blouse. Tears smeared mascara across her cheeks and her breathing was shallow.

"Hold on. I'm coming." Felicity glanced behind her. Noah was stationed in a crouch behind the desk, checking the parking lot. "Noah, Melanie's been hit. I need to cross the office to get to her." Doing so exposed her to the sniper if he was still out there. "Cover me."

He turned and caught her gaze. Held it. Just a moment, a heartbeat, but a thousand words neither of them could say passed between them. More than friendship. More than attraction. Love shimmered in the depths of his striking blue eyes. It punched her square in the gut and stole the little bit of air her lungs held onto.

Then he turned back to the parking lot. "On my mark." Noah paused, his gaze sweeping the immediate area. Felicity readied to spring forward when he gave the signal. "Go!"

She bolted across the office, half expecting a spray of bullets to riddle her body. To her relief, that didn't happen. Felicity slid to a halt next to Melanie. She yanked off her button-up shirt, revealing the white tank underneath, and tore the fabric to make bandages. Then she gently pried the other woman's hand away from the wound. "Let me see."

"I... don't want... to die." Melanie panted. Her

coloring was pale and her breathing rapid. Sweat beaded on her brow.

"No one is dying." Felicity pressed the makeshift bandages against the gunshot wound. "You've been shot, but it's just a graze. Some stitches and a bit of pain medication will fix you right up, but I need you to slow down your breathing. Can you do that for me?" Shock was deadly and from the rapid pace of Melanie's pulse flickering at her neck, she was heading straight in that direction. Felicity pressed harder on the wound to slow the bleeding. "I know the smoke makes breathing difficult, but you have to try."

Noah appeared at Felicity's side. "Looks like the sniper is gone. I've called the incident in and backup is en route. I have to check for more injured. From the looks of things, the shooter planted a bomb in the lobby."

"Go." Felicity's fears about more hurt civilians flared back to life. "I've got this."

His fingers brushed over her hair, and then he turned, racing through the smoke toward the front of the building.

Felicity sent up a prayer for Noah's safety and then turned her attention back to Melanie. Her coloring was getting better, but her breathing was still too fast. "You're doing great. Everything is going to be okay."

A roar punctuated her words. Felicity whirled in time to see a white van jump the curb and slam to a stop in front of the busted-out window. She reached for her weapon, but it was gone. She'd set it down to tend to

Melanie. Her gaze dropped to the carpet, but the gun was nowhere in sight.

Two masked men jumped out of the vehicle. Felicity jumped to her feet, attacking the first one with a solid kick to his kneecap. He yelped a curse as the other one closed in. A black bag descended over Felicity's head, casting her in darkness. She elbowed her attacker in the stomach and heard the air leave his body, but it didn't cause him to release his hold on her. His hands gripped her like a vise. Fabric filled her mouth as she desperately tried to gulp in air. Melanie's panicked screams vibrated her eardrums as the attacker attempted to drag Felicity toward the van.

She fought like a wildcat, training mingling with her need to survive. Once the men got her into that vehicle, she was dead. Felicity rammed her head against the face of the man holding her. Pain exploded along her skull as it collided with her attacker's chin. He stumbled back and the bruising grip on her arms loosened. She didn't waste a moment using that to her advantage. She shoved away from him.

"Police! Freeze!"

Noah's authoritative voice reached her ears as, once again, Felicity face-planted onto the carpet. Doors slammed as shots rang out, followed by tires squealing. Felicity sat up and frantically yanked at the dark hood covering her face. Sunshine and fresh air caressed her skin. Strong arms embraced her. Noah.

"Are you hit? Are you hurt?" He shifted the sweaty

hair away from her face with urgency, his gaze sweeping across her body, panic threaded in his voice. "Tell me."

"I'm okay." She sucked in a breath, holding on to his solid form. Her heart beat against her rib cage so violently, Felicity feared it might seize. She took a few precious seconds to suck in another breath and hold it before releasing the air slowly to ease her rapid pulse. "I'm okay."

Noah pulled her against him in a tighter embrace. Her head ached from the impact with her attacker. She sagged against him, breathing in the soothing scent of his cologne. The blood on her hands transferred to his shirt, sending a shock wave through her system.

Melanie.

The injured woman must be frightened out of her mind. Possibly in shock. Felicity pushed away from Noah, turning toward the bookcase. "We have to help Melanie."

The carpet was stained with blood, Felicity's gun tucked up against the edge of a row of books where it must've slid somehow in the confusion. Brooke's best friend, however, was gone.

Felicity's gaze traveled around the room, panic rising as the sound of the other woman's screams echoed like a bad dream in her mind. "Where's Melanie?" Her boots crunched glass as she took several steps toward the last place she'd seen the woman. Trembles shook her body despite the warm sunshine pouring over her skin.

Noah gently grabbed her arms, drawing her attention

to him. His hair was mussed and a scrape traveled the length of his powerful jaw. Approaching sirens wailed in the distance.

"They took her, Fee. Melanie's been kidnapped."

SEVENTEEN

Two hours later, the bullpen was buzzing with activity as Knoxville police joined forces with the sheriff's department and the Texas Rangers to investigate the attack at the bank. Noah carried a first aid kit into the break room, kicking the door closed behind him to block out the noise. His head was pounding. Some over-the-counter painkillers would help, but he needed to make sure Felicity was taken care of first. The stubborn woman had refused to go to the hospital.

She was seated at a table. A half-filled bottle of water rested in front of her, along with an unopened bag of crackers. Her hair was damp from a recent shower in the locker room, the faint freckles dancing across her nose visible without makeup, and her shoulders curved inward. Still, she offered a small smile at the sight of him. The curve of those lips, the way she tried to push through the worry and pain clouding her gaze, gut-punched him.

Felicity had no trouble reaching right inside his chest and grabbing hold of his heart.

"Finished giving your statement?" she asked.

"Yep." They'd been separated per protocol and provided their statements to investigating officers. Noah set the first aid kit on the table and reached for Felicity's wrist. He gently tugged her out of the chair into a standing position. Then he embraced her.

She sighed, nuzzling her face into the crook of his neck. His pulse settled. He brushed a kiss across the ridge of her hairline and breathed in the scent of her strawberry shampoo. She was here. She was alive. Noah didn't want to think about the terrifying moments during the shooting. Or the horror of rushing back into Melanie's office to find Felicity fighting for her life with a man twice her size. He'd nearly lost her today. More than once.

Felicity raised her face and then pushed to her tiptoes to kiss him. The moment their lips met, time stopped. Noah deepened the kiss, his heart saying what his mind couldn't fathom. He was falling in love with her and had been for a long time. Every threat drew attention to the depth of his feelings. There was no escaping it. No denying it.

And it terrified him right to the core.

Felicity had the ability to crush him. Losing her... would he survive it? He'd already been through so much pain, and now there was Harper to consider. Noah couldn't fall apart. He was a dad now. He'd pieced himself back together after Sally's death, but these feelings for Felicity had him balancing on a razor's edge.

LYNN SHANNON

Noah pulled back, ending the kiss, but kept his fore-head pressed against hers. He cupped her face in his hands. His thumbs gently ran over the silky skin along her cheeks. Her sharp inhale tempted him to kiss her again, but he resisted, instead lowering her back into the chair before opening the first aid kit. "Did you hear the news? Daniel is missing."

"Grady told me. According to his ex-wife, Daniel is on a fishing trip, but I doubt that's the case." She pushed aside the unopened box of crackers. "There were two attackers in the van. If we assume Gene was one of them, then the other could've been Daniel."

He nodded, ripping open an antiseptic wipe. "Hold still, this may sting." Noah gently dabbed at the cut along Felicity's temple. "The Rangers have sent out an alert to the local hospitals. Whoever attacked you is hurting right now after you smashed his kneecap." His mouth twitched. "Remind me never to make you angry."

She chuckled, and then the mirth slid from her expression. "I can't understand why they kidnapped Melanie. Is it because of what she knows about Daniel? Or is there more to it than that?"

"I don't know." Noah handed her a couple of over-the-counter pain meds and then took some for himself. He dry swallowed them. "Jax, Grady, and Tucker are in the conference room coordinating what we know so far. Let's go see what they've come up with."

Felicity took her own meds with a gulp of water. They stepped out of the break room into the chaos of the bull pen.

Judge Kurtis Ferguson was weaving his way through the desks behind an officer. His gaze landed on Felicity and an instant rage mottled his skin. He bolted for her on long strides. "You did this!"

Every head in the place turned toward them. Several officers rose from their chairs. Noah stepped in front of Felicity and placed a hand out to stop the judge. "Hold on there, sir."

"No, I won't." Kurtis drew to a halt. "How dare you!" He tried to peer around Noah to capture Felicity in his irate stare. His eyes were bloodshot, and it appeared he'd been crying from the ruddiness of his skin. "If you hadn't reopened Brooke's case, my wife would be at home with me right now. Instead, she's in the hands of criminals. Shot and bleeding out and—" His voice hitched as grief twisted his features. "Do you know what Triple 6 will do to her? Do you understand how many of them I've sent to prison?"

Sympathy softened Noah's tone. He understood Kurtis's heartache, but Melanie's kidnapping was not Felicity's fault and he wouldn't allow the judge to cast blame on her. "We're going to do everything in our power to bring Mrs. Ferguson home, sir."

Kurtis never shifted his gaze to Noah. He jutted a finger at Felicity. Spittle flew from the corner of his lips, and his hair was mussed and wild. "She's probably dead already!"

"Enough." Chief Garcia's booming command flew across the bullpen. He marched forward, his authoritative strides eating up the distance with ease, and then drew to a stop in front of Kurtis. "Judge Ferguson, if the men who kidnapped Melanie wanted her dead, they would've simply shot her. They have another agenda and we're working hard to uncover what that is. I've got law enforcement from three different agencies searching for your wife. We are doing everything humanly possible to find her, but we need your help." He gestured toward his office. "Come with me, sir."

Kurtis hesitated, then flew past Noah and Felicity toward the chief's office. His anger was like a hurricane sucking the air from the room. Noah registered every set of eyeballs on him and Felicity. He turned to face her and concern shot through him. She was ghost pale.

Taking her arm gently, he steered her toward the hallway leading to the conference room. Once they were away from prying eyes, he stopped. "Melanie's kidnapping was not your fault, Fee. The judge is upset and needs someone to blame—"

"I know, but that doesn't make this any easier." Frustration laced her voice. Felicity raised a hand to rub her forehead. "I keep thinking about the night Brooke died, trying to bring up any memory that would unlock this case, but I can't. I don't understand why I can't recall what happened."

"Hey." Noah cupped her shoulder, wanting to comfort her in any way possible. "Don't be so hard on yourself. You were a frightened fifteen-year-old kid. Brooke's murder was traumatizing. I don't blame you one bit for blocking it out."

She dropped her hand. "Has there been any word

about the shirt recovered from Jeremy? Was it Brooke's blood?"

"We're still waiting on the DNA. Tucker went to interview Jeremy yesterday but didn't find him." Noah was worried about the homeless man, but had bigger problems on his plate at the moment. "His tent was there, as was all his stuff, but no one at the camp has seen him since the day we visited. It's possible he's on a bender. Wouldn't be the first time. Jeremy's been known to disappear for days at a time."

"Makes it hard to interview him." Felicity dropped her hand. "Maybe it doesn't matter. Jeremy's an unreliable witness. Come on. Let's see what the team has uncovered about Daniel. Right now, he's our number one suspect."

EIGHTEEN

"I've combed through Daniel's financials, and he's got multiple accounts in his name, along with expenses that can't be explained through normal channels." Detective Jax Taylor turned his laptop screen around for Felicity. His dark hair was cropped close on the sides, but left longer on the top. A scar cut through the edge of his left eyebrow, giving him a rakish look that couldn't be undone by his clean shaven jawline. He looked like a cop who'd be more at home working undercover. "Daniel owns his home, drives a brand-new truck, and is making child support payments to his ex-wife. All of that combined is more than he makes as a sanitation worker."

"Could he have inherited money?" Felicity's vision blurred slightly as she scanned the reports on the laptop. The headache that'd been plaguing her since the attack was slowly abating, but exhaustion sucked the last reserves of her energy. She blinked to clear her vision.

Beside her, Noah frowned. No doubt he'd noticed her struggle to focus.

He gently pushed his untouched cup of coffee in her direction. Always the caregiver. She smiled gratefully before taking a long sip. The warmth spread through her.

"Daniel inherited some money when Brooke died, but that still doesn't explain all of his finances." Jax frowned. "In my opinion, Melanie was probably telling the truth. Daniel is involved in selling drugs."

"Would a guy making thousands selling drugs keep working at a sanitation company?" Felicity frowned. "It doesn't add up."

Jax shrugged. "You'd be surprised. Daniel may not want to draw attention to his side income, since the court would go through his finances for child support purposes." He pushed a printout across the table. "I also discovered a connection between Daniel and Gene. They spent a few days in county jail together. Roommates."

"That explains Gene's involvement."

"I'm working on getting a warrant right now to search Daniel's residence and property," Grady said from the other side of the conference table. The Texas Ranger typed furiously on the computer in front of him. His cowboy hat rested on the seat of a nearby chair and his blazer was thrown over the back. "The judge promised to look at it right away."

Felicity rose from her own chair, still holding on to the coffee, and started pacing the room. "Assuming Daniel killed his sister to keep her from turning him into the police for drug trafficking, which I'm willing to believe, there are still parts of this case that don't make sense. Why would Daniel kidnap Melanie? If he wanted to keep her from telling us about his drug business, wouldn't it make more sense to shoot her?"

"We can't assume Daniel is making the decisions. Maybe he's not." Noah leaned back in his chair. "Both Gene and Daniel probably work for Triple 6. The leader of the organization may have ordered Melanie to be kidnapped."

"But why?" Felicity blew out a breath. "Most criminal organizations steer clear of drawing law enforcement's attention. So far, they've attacked a Texas Ranger, shot at two law enforcement officers, bombed a bank, and kidnapped a judge's wife." She gestured to the packed bullpen behind the glass window of the conference room. "Multiple agencies are now working this case, searching for everyone potentially associated with Triple 6. That should be the last thing the leader wants."

The room was silent for a long time. Then Noah arched his brows. "Unless the leader is cleaning house."

Felicity paused midstep and turned to face him. "What do you mean?"

"The heat has been increasing on Triple 6 for a while. The Texas Rangers have been running an investigation into their organization. Even our small department has been chipping away at locating their drug hideouts. So far, only low-level individuals have been caught. Maybe this investigation into Brooke's murder spooked the leader, and he finally decided to get out of the business. Start fresh."

His theory made a lot of sense. Felicity's mind raced. "Melanie knows more than she told us at her office."

Noah nodded. "It would explain why she was kidnapped."

"The leader of Triple 6 needs her for something." Felicity spun toward Jax. "Can you dig into Ferguson's finances more? As the owner of a bank, Melanie would be a lot more adept at hiding illegal income." She inhaled sharply. "We also need a warrant to look through the bank's records. Triple 6 could be laundering money through the Knoxville Bank with Melanie's help."

Jax frowned. "Obtaining a warrant to search through the bank's records will be difficult unless we find solid proof there's a connection to Triple 6."

Frustration bubbled inside Felicity. They were so close, but theories weren't enough. They needed evidence. "Start with Daniel's bank account. Track where the payments or deposits come from and then see if there are any matching accounts funneling money to Melanie."

He turned his laptop around to face him and began typing quickly. "On it."

Grady, who'd been talking in a low voice on his cell phone, hung up. He stood and grabbed his cowboy hat. "The warrant came through. Let's roll. I'll call Tucker on the way and have him meet us there."

Felicity downed the last of the coffee and tossed the cup into the trash on her way out of the conference room. Noah drove with his turret lights flashing, but without the siren. Within fifteen minutes, they were pulling onto

Daniel's street. Every blind in his house was shut and the garage door was closed. Dark clouds hovered in the distance as an approaching storm blew toward them. Humidity threatened to wilt the last of Felicity's energy as she strapped on a bulletproof vest.

Grady marched toward them, gun in hand. "Tucker and I will enter the house at the rear. You guys take the front. A drug dog and his handler are on the way to help search the property."

Felicity nodded, pride knocking aside some of her fatigue. Grady had thought of everything. If Daniel was trafficking drugs, the K-9 would locate where he'd been hiding it, even if most of the stash had been moved. A drug dog's nose was sensitive and could pick up minute traces of illegal substances.

Several more officers pulled up in patrol cars. One was assigned to keep the neighbors a safe distance away from the house. A few went around the back with Grady and Tucker. Others joined Felicity and Noah as they approached the front door.

Sweat formed along the collar of her shirt. The weight of the bulletproof vest hurt her already aching muscles, but she ignored the pain. Felicity angled herself to the side of the doorframe and leveled her gun. She met Noah's gaze. "Go."

He pounded on the door. "Daniel Peterson, this is the police. We have a warrant to search the premises. Open up!"

No answer. Not surprising since he was reportedly on a fishing trip. Chances were, he'd actually skipped town. Felicity held her position, but Noah moved aside so the officers behind them could force the door open with a portable battering ram.

The wood splintered with a jarring crash. Noah kicked the broken door inward and went left. Felicity was directly on his heels, sweeping right. Her breath stalled as a familiar scent accosted her senses. Behind her, an officer gagged. The sound threatened to activate her own reflexes, but she swallowed the urge back down. "Noah."

He nodded in silent acknowledgement. The stench was unmistakable.

Death. Something was rotting in the house and had been for some time.

Air-conditioning kicked on, blowing against the sweat beaded along Felicity's bare skin. She shivered and adjusted the grip on her weapon. Her flashlight beam cut a path through the living room. Empty. The house was dark. Every shade was drawn and the approaching storm blocked the sunlight. The kitchen yawned to the left like a black hole. Felicity didn't want to continue. Duty and a need for answers forced her feet forward.

Lightning streaked across the sky as they traversed the dining room. The stench grew stronger the deeper into the house Felicity traveled. A doorway off the kitchen led to the garage. Noah indicated through hand signals that he wanted to search it. She nodded, taking up a protective stance to cover him. Her heart thundered against her rib cage.

He palmed the door handle. Lightning streaked across the sky again like a bad omen. It illuminated the determination etched on his strong features. Noah opened the door. The smell smacked Felicity in the face. It was overwhelming. Her stomach churned and bile threatened to rise in the back of her throat.

Her flashlight beam touched a tarp on the cement floor. It was the size of a body. On shaking steps, she followed Noah into the garage. A hand came into view. Male. Gray skin. Dirty nails and scraped knuckles. Daniel? Felicity's breathing shallowed as Noah bent down and, with the back of his flashlight, shifted the tarp away from the man's face.

She gasped. "That's not Daniel."

"No." Noah stood, his expression hard, but pain coated his words. "It's Jeremy."

NINETEEN

Night air wrapped around Noah as he traversed the path between the barn and his house. The horses had all been cared for by the ranch hands, but after dinner, he'd needed a few moments of solitude. Jeremy's murder weighed heavily on him. The homeless man had been shot twice in the chest, in a manner very similar to Brooke. Daniel was still missing along with his 9mm handgun. Why had he left Jeremy in his garage? The body had been wrapped in a tarp, indicating Daniel was in the process of disposing of it, but had aborted doing so for some reason.

Was it to help kidnap Melanie? There'd been two attackers at the bank, so that was a distinct possibility. Which led Noah to believe Daniel might be in charge of Triple 6. The more Jax dug into the other man's finances, the more money he uncovered. Brooke's brother had made millions over the years since her murder.

Thunder rumbled in the distance with the promise of

more storms. Already a front had moved through with more coming tonight and tomorrow. Movement to the left shifted Noah's attention. His hand went straight to the gun holstered at his side. A German shepherd appeared in the pool of light formed by the small solar lanterns along the pathway. His owner, Jason, a former Marine followed, accompanied by Nathan. The two men had volunteered to guard the property tonight.

Noah breathed out and let his hand drop. "Hey, guys. Everything okay?"

"Fine." Jason's posture was ramrod straight. A scar traversed his cheek and disappeared into his hairline. A war wound he'd earned in Afghanistan. His dog, Connor, also had a scar that cut through the fur along his side. Both of them had been involved in a bombing that'd ruined their military careers. "We're making the rounds. Logan and Kyle will be here later to join in."

"I can't tell you how much I appreciate it." Noah, worried for Felicity's safety, insisted she stay on his ranch in the guest room. The house had a top-notch security system, but having a group of military men guarding the property was added insurance.

"No need to thank us." Nathan squared his shoulders. "Knoxville is our home too. We want to keep it safe." A smile twitched his lips. "Not to mention that protecting Felicity keeps me in my wife's good graces. Cassie is fiercely loyal. I practically had to tie the woman down to keep her from coming over here to protect Felicity too."

Jason snorted. "That's what happens when you

marry a strong-willed woman. I would know." He arched his brows at Noah. "Don't worry if our wives show up tomorrow after church with casseroles and baked goods. They have a tendency to adopt anyone in danger. Addison's been coordinating the effort since this afternoon."

Addison was Jason's wife. The couple had an adorable baby boy together.

Noah grinned back. "You and your wives are always welcome. Aunt Imogene loves having visitors. She'll be over the moon to have more mouths to feed. Speaking of which, there's food and fresh coffee in the kitchen. Be sure to help yourselves anytime."

The men chatted a bit longer and then Noah continued on to the house. He stepped inside to discover Imogene pulling out a batch of freshly baked rolls from the oven. The scent of yeast bread mingled with home-made tomato sauce. A lasagna rested on the counter. Noah's stomach growled. He washed his hands in the sink and then kissed his aunt's cheek. "The food smells amazing. Where's Harper?"

"Playing in the living room." Imogene snagged his hand before he could go around the corner. "Wait, you have to see this." She lifted a finger to her lips to indicate Noah should be quiet and then tiptoed silently around the doorframe.

Noah followed, curiosity getting the better of him. Milo was snoozing in the corner of the living room, and with a few more steps, Harper came into view. She was on the floor playing with a stack of blocks. Felicity, dressed in yoga pants and a soft T-shirt, sat facing her.

Both of them wore princess crowns. They discussed the colors and shapes on the blocks as they built a tower. Noah's heart melted at the sweet tone Felicity used with his little girl. And the way Harper looked at her... like Felicity was a superhero. It was a sentiment Noah understood well. He adored the beautiful woman too.

"They've been playing for the last hour," Imogene whispered. "It's too cute."

Harper knocked the tower over with one blow. Felicity's expression morphed into one of exaggerated surprise and appreciation. "Wow! You're so strong!" She tickled Harper and peals of laughter filled the room. "I'm going to build the tower again. Don't you dare knock it over."

Felicity started stacking blocks and Harper immediately toppled them. More tickling and laughter followed. Noah's chest squeezed tight as a wash of emotions swept over him too muddled and confusing to sort out. He didn't even know where to begin. Felicity had nearly died today. Had escaped death several times over the last few days. Was it wise to allow Harper to get closer to her? Was it smart for Noah to have opened the door to any kind of relationship by kissing Felicity?

Imogene must've sensed his turbulence, because she tugged him back into the kitchen. Once the door was shut behind them, she whirled to face him. "What's the matter?"

"I..." Noah scraped a hand through his hair. He wasn't one to discuss his feelings, but Imogene had been his rock for decades. She'd nursed him through the loss of his parents and again through the pain of Sally's death. If anyone could understand the twist in his thoughts, it was her. "I've created a mess and don't know what to do next."

He turned and sank into a chair. "Felicity and I kissed. I think... I think I'm in love with her and the idea of that terrifies me. Felicity is being hunted by a killer, but even after this case is over, she has a dangerous job. What's going to happen if she dies? I've lost so many people in my life and now there's Harper to consider. Is it really a good idea for her to get closer to Felicity?"

"That's fear talking."

"Darn right it is." His fingers curled into his palm. "I know what it's like to lose someone you love. How painful and heartbreaking it can be. Don't I have a right to be scared?"

"Of course you do, child." She pulled out a chair and joined him at the table. "But you can't protect Harper from heartache. Doing so would require her never loving anyone, and I don't think you want her going through life like that."

No, he didn't. Noah released a long exhale. "Felicity's the first person who ever made me want to love again after losing Sally, and I tried not being scared of my feelings, but... what if I'm not capable of doing it?"

"Turn to the Lord and ask for strength." Imogene placed a hand on his arm. "God doesn't make mistakes. He has perfect timing. Always. He's brought you and Felicity together in this moment for a reason. Think about it, Noah. Other than me, who understands the depth of your loss? Felicity. She knew your parents, held your hand on the day of their funeral, and has supported you through the ups and downs of your life since. Including your marriage, the birth of Harper, and Sally's death. She's your best friend."

The wisdom of her observations sank into Noah. Felicity was the only other person—besides Imogene—who had supported him through everything. She knew him. Understood him in a way no one else did and there was comfort in that.

"I know you're scared," Imogene continued. "But that's when you need God the most. Replace your fear with faith. Trust that He has a plan for you, one that includes happiness and love."

He wanted to but wasn't quite ready to surrender completely. "I have some praying to do."

TWENTY

The next morning, Felicity eased the screen door shut behind her as she stepped onto the back porch of Imogene's home. Dew coated the grass, and the air was heavy with the scent of pine and fresh earth. Raindrops peppered the wood, exposed to the elements beyond the shelter of the roof. The sky was moody. Clouds drifted quickly, and a breeze ruffled the edges of Felicity's ponytail. One good thing about the rain was a drop in temperatures.

The house inside was quiet. Imogene, Amber, and Harper had all gone to church service. Felicity had also wanted to attend, but after the bank bombing last night, determined it'd be safer for everyone if she stayed on the ranch. The last thing she wanted was to put more innocent civilians at risk.

She sipped her coffee. Her dreams had been haunted by images from the last few days, intermingled with brief pieces of memories from the night Brooke was murdered.

Felicity had woken and immediately written her impressions. She glanced over the page. The porch swing rocked gently when she pushed it with her foot.

"Morning." Noah strolled across the yard. He was dressed in jeans and mud-covered cowboy boots. A soft T-shirt molded to every one of his powerful muscles, his hair was mussed, and a beard shadowed his jaw. He must've been caring for the horses in the barn. Milo trotted at his side.

Felicity's heart stuttered at the sight of Noah and then took rapid flight. The man had the power to undo her with just a glance. It was heady. Intoxicating. She wanted to drown in the warmth in his eyes and forget about every ounce of trouble plaguing her. But that wasn't possible. Not while there was a killer on the loose and a woman missing. "Any word on Melanie?"

Noah's expression darkened. "Nothing yet."

Disappointment pinched her. Milo plopped down on the porch with a sigh and promptly went to sleep. The Lab pup was clearly exhausted. "You tuckered him out."

"Finally." Noah's boots thumped against the porch steps. "It only took all morning."

She chuckled and then forced her gaze back down to the paper clutched in her hands. "I had dreams. About Brooke. I wrote some of my impressions, but I'm not sure how accurate they are."

He joined her on the porch swing. "Let's hear it."

"Voices arguing." Felicity set her coffee cup down on the side table. "Two, at least. Maybe more. Brooke shouted something along the lines of 'You can't do this.'

And then the sound of gunshots." Panic swelled inside of her, as real as the day Brooke was murdered, but she battled it back. She was safe. Here with Noah. He wouldn't let anyone hurt her. "I remember hearing a man's voice. I don't know whose though."

"That fits with our current theory that Daniel killed his sister."

Felicity nodded and folded the paper. She bit her lip. "And Jeremy?"

"I think he witnessed the crime, just like you did. The DNA came back on the shirt this morning. It was Brooke's. I suspect Jeremy attempted to provide first aid, but you interrupted him. Maybe Jeremy heard the killer coming back?"

She nodded. "Whatever happened, he was trying to shield me."

"Agreed. Jeremy must've hid too; otherwise I think the killer would've shot him on the spot. Chances are, he didn't know about either of you until after the fact. Since Jeremy was paranoid, the police wouldn't have taken him seriously if he'd come forward. There was no reason to kill him."

"And now?"

"Now there's you." Noah wrapped an arm around her shoulder and pulled her closer. "Your memories combined with Jeremy's may have been enough to iden-tify the killer. Daniel's worried. He's cleaning house, probably getting ready to leave the country once all the loose ends are tied up."

"You're convinced he's the leader of Triple 6?"

"It's looking more and more like it. The drug dogs Grady had run through the property found traces of opioids, and the more Jax digs into Daniel's finances, the more he discovers. Apparently, Daniel owns several shell corporations that own land adjoining the state park. A lot of drug dealers use state parks to shield their activities since there aren't enough rangers to patrol the areas." Noah frowned. "We're working on searching all the known properties for Melanie. Nothing yet."

It all fit, but something about the theory bugged her. Felicity couldn't distinguish what though. "I'd like to go over all the evidence in the case file again from the beginning. We may be overlooking something that could help."

"Okay." Noah tugged her closer. "But first, we're going to sit here and enjoy this morning. Just for a second."

She sighed and leaned into his embrace. He smelled of horse and hay, but it wasn't unpleasant. Strangely enough, it was comforting. "I'm sorry about Jeremy." Responsibility and guilt twisted her insides. "I should've realized he was in danger."

"Don't beat yourself up. I missed it too." He was quiet for several heartbeats. "His paranoia... it was a difficult disease for him to handle. I would never have wished him harm and Jeremy didn't deserve what happened to him, but I pray he's at peace now."

"So do I."

Noah brushed a kiss across the top of her head. He reached around and plucked her coffee cup from the side table, taking a sip before handing it to her. The intimacy of the action wasn't lost on Felicity. Tenderness swept through her. She tilted her head back to see his face. The strong jaw line and straight nose. His perfectly formed lips.

As if reading the train of her thoughts, Noah's hand lifted. His fingers brushed the sensitive skin along her cheekbone. He dipped his head and kissed her. Just a light brush of his lips against hers, but Felicity's pulse skyrocketed.

Noah backed away and smiled. "I'd kiss you more, but Nathan and Jason are on patrol again. No need to give them a show."

Her cheeks flushed. Felicity's gaze shot to the yard. There was no sign of the two men, but that didn't mean they weren't close by. Military guys knew how to stay hidden. "I feel bad they were tramping around in the rain last night."

"They took shifts. Aunt Imogene made sure they had plenty of coffee and food. She also set up cots in one of the spare bedrooms." Noah pushed the swing with his foot to send them rocking. "But I'm thinking of throwing a party after this is all over. Just to show my appreciation."

"That sounds nice."

He took the coffee from her hand and sipped it. Silence descended between them, broken only by the faint patter of raindrops and birdsong. Felicity sighed. The peacefulness of the moment stole over her. She tried to remind herself not to get too attached. To Noah or this land. But it was difficult to deny the yearning in her heart. Playing with Harper last night had driven home just how much she wanted to be a part of their lives. She wasn't just falling in love with Noah. She'd fallen in love with his daughter too.

A part of her desperately wanted to talk about her feelings. Another part was terrified to. Felicity bit her lip, indecision warring within her. Before she could decide how to handle it, Noah cleared his throat. "I've been praying this morning."

She glanced up at him again. "About the case?"

"No." He scoffed. "Although that should've been at the forefront of my mind. Trouble is, I'm finding it harder and harder to concentrate on anything except you."

She froze as her mind went blank. Noah licked his lips nervously, his fingers playing with the edge of her sleeve. The brush of his hand against her bare skin, coupled with his sudden declaration, was beyond distracting. Felicity backed away from his embrace. "I don't understand."

Noah swallowed. "Forget it. We agreed to postpone discussing us until after the case was over—"

"No." She tried to meet his gaze, but he avoided her eyes. Her stomach sank. "You and I have always been good about tackling hard issues. Letting this linger between us has been necessary, but with Chief Garcia and Grady taking over the investigation, it's a good time to talk. So let's do it. Finish what you were about to say."

He was quiet for a long moment. Noah's gaze drifted across the pasture, and he absently played with the end of his ring finger. "When Sally died, I was determined never to become involved in another romantic relationship. You remember. I was devastated."

She remembered. Noah had loved Sally with all of his heart. It'd taken months before he even smiled again. Caring for Harper had helped him keep going, but his pain had been raw.

Was Noah about to tell her that he couldn't move on? Felicity's gut clenched tight, and she braced herself for him to say the words. No crying. She'd known this was a possibility right from the get-go. Felicity breathed out. "What you and Sally had was very special."

"It was." Noah's voice was soft. He smiled absently. "Aunt Imogene was right. You're the only person I can think of who would understand." Now he met her gaze. "I didn't think I could ever be with someone else, Fee, but I was wrong. I'm falling in love with you."

The words stunned her. "You love me?"

He nodded. "I've been too scared to admit it because the idea of losing you... it's terrifying."

Fear gripped her then. Ice cold and fierce, it stole her breath. Everything she wanted was right there, within reach, but she didn't know how to stretch out her hand. Instead, she rose to her feet. Took several steps across the porch to the railing. Raindrops peppered her bare skin, causing goosebumps to rise. "I can't guarantee something won't happen to me, Noah."

"Of course you can't. That's why I've been praying. A lot. I have to put my faith in God and trust that He'll guide me through whatever comes our way." The swing creaked as Noah rose. "Fee. Look at me."

She turned on her heel. Her heart shot into her throat, stealing her breath. Noah stood tall and strong and capable. He was everything she'd ever wanted in a man. His kindness and caring were unmatched. He made her laugh, comforted her when things were bad, and took responsibility for his actions. And yet the distance between them was like a gulf. Was she good enough?

Trust in God.

Once again, Cassie's advice rang in Felicity's head. Noah was essentially saying the same thing. She should lean into her faith and grasp this happiness with both hands. But knowing what she *should* do and actually doing it were two different things. She breathed in once. Twice. Noah had taken a leap by sharing his fears with her. It was only right she do the same.

Felicity straightened her spine. "My career is my life. It's guided my choices since I graduated from college. I don't know any other way to be." She chewed on the inside of her lip. "My dad loved me, but I spent a lot of my childhood feeling alone because his career was his priority. I want a family, Noah—" Emotion clogged her throat and she struggled to keep ahold of herself. "I'm falling in love with you too. But you may find being in a relationship with me disappointing."

"No, Fee." He moved closer and reached for her hand. Placed it over his heart. The steady beat thumped against her palm. "For starters, you could never be a disappointment. I know being raised by a single dad was lonely, but you guys didn't have anyone other than each other. Harper and I have family who love and support us.

We aren't expecting you to be our everything." His mouth quirked up at the corners. "Nor would I ever want you to give up your job. Law enforcement is your calling, same as me. I know a little something about how difficult it can be to balance home and work life."

Some of the weight pressing down on her lifted as hope blossomed. "Do you..." She lifted her gaze to his. "You think we can do this?"

"Yes. I'm not promising it'll be easy. We're both going to make mistakes along the way. Forgiveness is part of the bargain." He trailed a finger along her hairline. "Honesty too. Whatever fears we have, we share them with each other. And God. Doing that will help us know what steps to take."

She smiled. "Trust in God."

"Yes. And each other." He met her gaze. "I love you, Felicity."

"I love you too."

Noah tilted closer to kiss her, but his cell phone rang, interrupting their special moment. He growled and yanked it from his pocket before glancing at the screen. "It's my aunt." He held up a finger. "One minute."

He answered. Felicity couldn't hear Imogene's words, but her panicked tone filtered from the phone's speaker. She crossed the porch to Noah's side.

Blood leeched from his face. He met her gaze. An indescribable feeling gripped her as she registered the terror in his eyes. "What happened?"

"Harper's missing."

TWENTY-ONE

"We're going to find her."

Felicity pressed harder on the gas pedal, pushing Noah's vehicle to the maximum. Trees whipped by in a blur. Rain tapped against the windshield, but darker clouds in the distance promised a coming storm. The county was under a tornado watch. She gripped the steering wheel harder as wind pushed against the Tahoe. In the passenger seat beside her, Noah was silent. His gaze was locked on the road, the muscles in his body and jaw so tight, it was a wonder he didn't snap in two.

She spared a glance in his direction. Fear, worry, and responsibility swirled inside her with the force of a hurricane. Harper wasn't her daughter. She loved the little girl, but Felicity didn't dare dream an ounce of what she was feeling compared to what Noah was currently going through. He'd lost so many people in his life. And this was his daughter. *His daughter.*

She tapped the brake to make a turn onto Main

Street. "Lord, please keep Harper safe. Give us the wisdom and ability to find her quickly. Guide our movements that we may be smart, capable, and clearheaded."

"Amen." Noah sucked in a shuddering breath. "How did I miss this, Fee?" He pounded against the dash. "I should've had someone protecting them."

"It's not your fault. There was no indication your family was in danger."

The killer was after Felicity. Taking Harper was a distraction. Or a lure. Felicity wasn't sure which yet, but she was going to do everything in her power to bring that little girl home to her daddy.

The church loomed as Felicity skated through several red lights. She barely hit the brakes again while turning into the parking lot. The Tahoe screeched to a stop near the front door. Several Knoxville Police Department cruisers were already on site. Noah sprang from the vehicle and raced inside. Felicity quickly followed.

Grady met them in the entranceway. The Texas Ranger had set up a small command center at the front desk. A map of the church along with one of the town had been hastily taped to the wall. His cowboy hat had been thrown to the side and Grady's hair was mussed as if he'd been running his hands through it.

"Harper was in the playroom with the other kids but asked to use the bathroom." Grady's tone was clipped, but his eyes held sympathy. Felicity understood it. Her colleague was a father. He had an adopted little girl and a three-month-old baby. Every lawman she'd ever met feared the job would someday touch their family. "A teacher took her. They were ambushed in the ladies' room by an unknown assailant. He knocked out the teacher and took Harper."

"Cameras?" Noah barked out.

"The church has a few over the front doors and the parking lot, but the kidnapper used an interfering device to scramble the feed. There aren't any cameras inside the offices or children's play area. Officers are gathering video from every store on Main Street in the hopes that we'll get a lead on the vehicle the kidnapper was driving. More officers are combing the alley behind the church, searching for any evidence that may lead us to Harper."

The kidnapping had been planned. Carefully. Was Daniel behind it? As the leader of Triple 6 and Brooke's killer, it seemed likely. But Felicity couldn't understand why he'd go to such lengths to nab Noah's daughter. It didn't make sense.

"I want to talk to the teacher." Noah's expression was stone hard. "Is she here?"

"Yes. She's with your aunt in a classroom down the hall."

Felicity touched Noah's arm briefly. "I'm going to view the security feed from the last few days. The killer scrambled the video today, but whoever is behind this had to stake out the church beforehand."

Grady pointed to a small room near the entrance. "In there."

Felicity nodded. The electronics room was small, but ruthlessly organized. A security guard watched a live video feed of the parking lot. He glanced up as she came in and she flashed her badge. "I'd like to review the video from the last several days."

Fifteen minutes later, she was scrolling through footage from an hour before the kidnapping. The security guard requested to get a cup of coffee and disappeared from the room. Felicity barely heard the door click behind him. Her gaze was locked on the screen, watching parishioners arrive for church service.

She spotted Imogene in a pantsuit with Amber. The teen had pulled her hair back in a braid. Harper was nestled between them, cute as a button in a frilly white dress and Mary Jane shoes. Felicity's chest tightened, but she shuttered the emotions. No good would come by falling apart.

She kept moving the tape forward. About fifteen minutes before the kidnapping, the screen became static. That must've been when the kidnapper started scrambling the feed. But no one had recently arrived in the parking lot.

The kidnapper had already been in the building.

Felicity rolled the tape back and, this time, watched every single parishioner as they walked through the parking lot. Her heart skipped a beat as a familiar individual stepped out of an old Chevy truck parked close to the alley.

No. It couldn't be.

Her cell phone rang. The number on screen wasn't familiar. Still, Felicity answered while searching for a way to zoom in on the individual in the footage. She had to be sure before telling Grady and Noah. Sending them down a rabbit hole could cost Harper her life. "Ranger Capshaw."

"You've got two minutes to do exactly as I say, or the little girl dies."

Felicity's muscles froze. The voice on the phone was muffled and distinctly male. "Daniel?"

"Who I am doesn't matter. Your actions do. We're down to one minute, thirty seconds."

She whirled out of the chair and went to the door. Stuck her head out. No one was in the hallway or at the temporary command center. "How do I know you have Harper?"

Her phone dinged with a text message. A video. Felicity quickly pulled it up. Harper lay on a beige carpet. She was unconscious, but her chest was moving. Alive. Relief was short-lived though. She pressed the phone to her ear. Anger colored her words. A deep-seated rage Felicity hadn't known she was capable of. "Don't you dare hurt Harper."

"Don't make me. There's a truck at the edge of the church parking lot. Keys are in the cup holder, instructions taped to the visor. Leave your cell phone and slip away without anyone noticing." His tone was hostile and chilling. "Be careful, Felicity. If I suspect you've disobeyed my orders, I will slice this little girl's throat."

The threat was real. Felicity felt it in her bones.

"Thirty seconds. I've tapped into the church security feed and I'll know if you try to trick me."

She had no way of knowing if that claim was true. Felicity couldn't draw in a full breath. "If you do anything to Harper, I will hunt you to the end of the earth."

"You control her fate. If I were you, I'd get a move on."

Her phone dinged with another message. A photo. Harper was still sleeping on the same beige carpet, but a hunting knife pressed against the smooth column of her sweet throat. Felicity literally saw red. She clenched her teeth. "I'll do as you say."

"Hurry up. Twenty seconds."

TWENTY-TWO

It was his worst nightmare.

Noah had a stranglehold on his emotions, but barely. It seemed bizarre that less than half an hour ago, he and Felicity were declaring their feelings for each other. Now the family he'd started to envision was in danger. His little girl—his baby—had been kidnapped.

"I'm so sorry." The volunteer teacher, a grandmother named Barbara Flanagan, twisted tissues in her wrinkled hands. Her gray hair was speckled with blood from a wound on her forehead, and a small lump was forming. Her skin was turning black and blue at an alarming rate. "One minute, Harper and I were entering the bathroom, and the next, I was on the floor."

Imogene wrapped a set of paper towels around an ice pack and pressed it to Barbara's head. "It's not your fault." She gave Noah a beseeching look that was filled with heartbreak. "No one blames you."

"Of course not." Noah caught Tucker's eye. The

detective had initially interviewed Mrs. Flanagan and was currently coordinating a more thorough search for Harper with Grady. "Get some paramedics in here."

"No, I don't want—"

"Ma'am, you've been attacked and ice will make that knot on your forehead better, but it's best to have a medical professional check you out." He leaned forward. "Mrs. Flanagan, I need you to think back on the moments before the attack. Did you notice anyone in the hallway? Or did the person who attacked you say anything?"

Fresh tears swelled in her eyes. "No. I already told Officer Colburn everything I know."

"I understand. It's difficult to answer these questions repeatedly, but any detail can help." Urgency crimped his insides, but Noah kept his tone calm. "Do me a favor. Close your eyes, ma'am."

Her brow wrinkled slightly, but then she did as he asked. Noah leaned forward. "We're going to walk through it one step at a time. You left the classroom with Harper. Were you holding her hand?"

"Yes. She was singing *Mary Had A Little Lamb*. Her smile was so infectious—" She pressed tissues to her mouth.

Noah took her other hand. "It's okay. As you walked down the hall toward the bathroom, did you notice anything out of the ordinary?"

Barbara sucked in a breath. "No. I pushed the door open to the ladies' room and..." Her eyes snapped open. "There was something. A flash of color inside the classroom across from the restrooms. Someone was there. A woman. I just got the barest glimpse of her before she disappeared around the doorjamb."

A woman? It would make sense. No one remembered seeing either Daniel or his criminal friend Gene hanging around the church. Did they rope someone else into doing their dirty work? That could explain how someone slipped into and out of the daycare area without a problem. A strange man would've been noticed. A woman, on the other hand, wouldn't have been seen as a potential threat.

Grady joined them. He had a pad and pen in his hand. "Can you describe the woman you saw?"

"No." Her gaze drifted away as if she was reviewing the incident in her mind. "I just remember seeing the flash of a blue skirt. I never saw her face." Barbara's attention jumped back to Noah. "Does that help?"

Something was better than nothing. "It helps a lot."

Paramedics appeared in the doorway. Grady waved them forward. They immediately got to work examining Barbara, and Noah cleared out of the way so they had more room. He hugged his aunt. "Stay with her. I'll contact you the minute we know something more."

Without a word, he and Grady slipped from the room. Noah headed for the electronics room at the end of the hall. Surveillance footage could help. "We've been looking for Daniel or Gene, but based on Mrs. Flanagan's statement, the kidnapper was in the daycare before the camera feed was interrupted." His stride lengthened. "Maybe Felicity has found something—"

The door to the electronics room was open and the

chair in front of the computer screen was empty. Noah slid to a stop, his stomach dropping to his feet when he noticed Felicity's badge and cell phone sitting on the table. A note in her scrawled handwriting rested on the keyboard. "I'm sorry. Harper's life depended on it. Look at the footage."

Grady snatched the note from Noah's hand. "What does this mean?"

"The kidnapper contacted her." He slammed a fist down on the table. "Taking Harper was a way to force Felicity into a trap."

"No. Felicity wouldn't submit to a kidnapper's demand or go somewhere without backup. She's smarter than that."

Noah unlocked Felicity's cell with her PIN code and an image popped on the screen. The last text message she'd received was a photo. His daughter—his precious little girl—lying on a carpet in a nondescript room with a knife to her throat. His heart stopped even as his knuckles turned white. Noah showed Grady the image. "Trust me, she did whatever the kidnapper told her to."

An uncharacteristic swear flew from Grady's mouth. Noah shared the sentiment. He thought nothing could be worse than having his child kidnapped, but seeing this image and knowing the woman he loved was now also in danger...

Please God. Please. Protect them. I can't lose them both.

"Felicity said to look at the footage. What footage?" Grady moved the mouse for the computer. The monitor popped on, displaying an image from earlier in the day according to the time stamp. "What are we supposed to be looking for?"

"The cameras are still running. Let's see how Felicity leaves."

Grady quickly accessed the correct time frame. Felicity hurried out a side door and crossed the parking lot on determined strides to a rusted-out truck near the alley. She hopped inside. A moment later, she drove off.

Noah leaned on the desk. "Can you make out the license plate on that vehicle?"

"No, but I'd like to know how it got here." Grady used the controls to work backward to earlier in the day. The footage rolled on at an increased speed.

"There." Noah's heart pumped overtime when he spotted the vehicle drive into the parking lot. Grady slowed the footage down. Both of them kept their gazes locked on the truck. A woman exited. She wore a blue skirt and blouse, her dark hair flowing around her shoulders. "Barbara said the woman in the classroom opposite the ladies' room wore a blue skirt. That has to be her. But she doesn't look familiar... Wait a minute."

Something about her *was* familiar. He ignored her hair color and body shape, focusing on her gait, which was harder to disguise. Noah blinked. "It's Melanie Ferguson."

Grady's head whipped toward him. "What? Are you sure?"

"Roll it back." He studied the woman as she exited the vehicle and walked toward the church. It was definitely Melanie. She was in disguise, but it was her. Noah's hands balled into fists. "I'm sure. It's her."

"That doesn't make sense. Why would Melanie kidnap your daughter?"

Noah's mind raced, desperately trying to put all the pieces together. There was only one explanation that made any sense. "She's the leader of Triple 6. Or at least associated in some way. A criminal organization like that would need to funnel money through legitimate means. What better way than to launder money using a family-owned bank?" He blew out a breath. "Felicity mentioned it to Jax yesterday, but we didn't have any evidence linking Melanie with Triple 6 in order to obtain a warrant to look at the bank's records."

"How does Daniel tie in? And Gene?"

"They work for her." Noah whipped out his cell phone and called Jax. The detective answered on the first ring. "I need to know about any property Melanie or her husband own. It could be under a corporation's name. We're looking for something remote, but accessible."

He didn't ask for any explanation. "On it."

"Hold on." Grady paced the room. "If Melanie is behind Triple 6, she went to a lot of trouble to make herself look like a victim. She's not the kind of person to up and disappear from her life. Not with her kind of money. So why would she have her lackeys shoot and kidnap her?" He paused midstep. "And why would Daniel leave a dead body in his house for the police to find?"

Noah caught on to what he was saying. "He

wouldn't. Melanie is cleaning house. She needs someone to blame. A fall guy."

Grady fisted his hands. "We've been all over every property Daniel owns."

"Maybe he doesn't own it." He lifted the phone back to his ear. "Scratch that, Jax. I need to know about any property Daniel's ex-wife owns. Something she inherited or had while they were married. Again, it'll be remote but accessible."

Noah sent up a silent prayer as he fled the electronics room, heading for his vehicle. Grady was right on his heels. The sound of Jax's keyboard clicking came over the line. "I've got something."

Hope sprang in Noah's heart even as his pace increased. "Send me the address."

TWENTY-THREE

Rain beat a steady drum against the roof of the ancient truck as Felicity navigated the muddy dirt road leading to God knew where. The directions on the small piece of paper tucked in the visor were easy enough to follow, but it'd taken over thirty minutes to arrive at this remote location. If she'd been followed, it wasn't obvious. She'd passed several gas stations along the way, and had been tempted to pull over and call Noah using someone else's cell phone but resisted. The kidnapper could've placed a tracker on the vehicle. Felicity wouldn't do anything to risk Harper's life.

She prayed the note left on the desk back at the church was enough of a clue for Noah to follow. He was smart. So was Grady. They'd figure it out. The question was: how long would it take? Backup could be fifteen minutes away, or it could be hours before they put the pieces together.

Noah. Her heart ached thinking of him. Hours ago,

he'd declared his love and shared his fears about losing another person he cared about. Felicity had no illusions about the danger she was walking into. The chances of making it out alive were slim to none. Her only saving grace was Harper's survival. The kidnappers had taken the little girl to lure Felicity to this wooded property. Hopefully, once they had what they wanted, they'd let Harper go.

It was a long shot. A desperate move. But one Felicity had to take.

She wouldn't be able to live with herself otherwise.

Tree branches scraped the sides of the truck as the overgrowth narrowed the muddy lane. The screeching sound tangled with Felicity's frayed nerves. Her heart thundered against her rib cage. She tightened her hold on the wheel. "Lord, my life is in Your hands. Harper's too. I pray You will help me protect this innocent child from further harm. Return her to Noah. He needs her."

A strong sense of calm and purpose took hold of Felicity. She leaned into it. There was no room for doubt. Or fear. She *would* rescue Harper. That was all that mattered.

The trees parted, revealing a ramshackle farmhouse. Busted windows gaped like empty eye sockets. Overgrown vines clambered up the side of the broken front porch and onto the roof. A listing barn, faded by time and the changing weather, sat a short distance away.

A chill swept over Felicity. She killed the engine on the old truck but didn't exit the vehicle. Thunder rumbled across the sky.

The place looked abandoned. Was Harper inside? It was possible the kidnappers held the girl in a different location. Felicity scanned the property, but there were no other vehicles on the premises. Maybe they were in the barn. Or hidden in the woods.

She flipped the slider for the interior cab light so it wouldn't turn on when the door was opened and then scooted across the bench seat to the passenger side. Felicity slipped from the vehicle. She quietly closed the door and crept into the woods. She'd arrived on the premises. They'd know that if they were tracking her vehicle. But she wouldn't surrender. Not without verifying Harper's safety.

Rain instantly soaked her. It dribbled down her hair and into the collar of her shirt, icing her skin despite the humid air. Felicity palmed her weapon. She scooted along the edge of the trees, watching for any sign of life. Nothing stirred. What game were the kidnappers playing? Had they rigged the house to explode the moment she entered?

Fear shot straight through her core. The bomb at the bank had been a simple homemade device. Anyone with internet access and some materials from the local hardware store could've built it, which meant they could make more than one. The other option was that someone was hiding in the house, waiting for her to enter.

Indecision warred within her. Felicity moved to the rear of the house. The back door was missing, the interior pitch-black. She scanned the surrounding area one more time but didn't have the sense someone was hiding and watching nearby. Felicity kept moving until she'd circled the house. Now it was time to peek inside the windows. If Harper was inside, hopefully she'd be visible.

The damp ground sucked at Felicity's boots as she ran across the open space to the side of the house. The first set of windows led to the kitchen. Cabinet doors were missing and the ancient refrigerator hung open. She kept moving, keeping close to the building for protection, her senses on high alert for any signs of movement. Peeking in the next set of windows stopped her heart.

Harper. The little girl lay on the same beige carpeting as in the photos. Her curly hair had fallen from its previously neat ponytail and spilled around her face like a halo. Her eyes were closed. Drugged? Probably. With any luck, the sweet baby wouldn't remember any of the kidnapping. There was no sign of blood on her small body. Something Felicity was grateful for.

Her instinct was to rush inside the room, but training kept her feet planted. Once more, she searched the surrounding area for anyone lurking nearby.

Nothing.

The glass in the window had broken a long time ago. Felicity shoved against the weathered wood. The sash slid up high enough for her to slip through. She quickly lifted her body onto the sill and then dropped into the room. Water dripped from her clothes onto the carpet, forming dark spots. Mold and some other scent she couldn't identify swept across her nostrils. Felicity wanted to rush to Harper's side, pick up the girl, and escape this horrible place.

Not yet. She adjusted the hold on her weapon, her gaze shooting to the hallway. With the sky darkened by the storm and the electricity in the house out, visibility was poor. She sensed another person's presence. Her brain registered the strange scent she couldn't initially place.

Cologne. A man's cologne.

Where was he?

A closet was tucked along the far wall of the bedroom. The door was closed. Checking it would allow someone to sneak in from the hallway. Going to the hallway would give someone in the closet an opening. Either way, she couldn't clear both without putting herself at risk. Her mind whipped through the options in half a heartbeat. There was only one choice.

She turned toward Harper. Felicity dropped to one knee and reached for the little girl's wrist as if to check for a pulse. The air behind her shifted. Anticipating the attack, she whirled around as Daniel rushed her from the dark hallway. Felicity fired. Her bullet slammed into his center mass and he stumbled back, but no blood bloomed on his shirt. Instead, he swung wide with the baseball bat in his hands.

She ducked, but the weapon connected with her shoulder. Pain exploded in her body. The gun slipped from her numb fingers to the ground. Daniel kept coming. She barely dodged a second swing at her head. Felicity lowered her shoulder and rushed the man.

Her body collided with something unnaturally hard. A bulletproof vest. Felicity registered the protection even

LYNN SHANNON

as her mind calculated the options available. Daniel growled as he grappled with her in an attempt to stay on his feet. His grip was bruising. The roar of her heartbeat filled her ears. Training and instinct took over. Felicity used her free hand to punch him square in the groin.

He let out an explicative and crumpled to the ground. She ripped the baseball bat from his hand.

The sound of a round chambering came from the doorway. Felicity whirled around, already raising the bat to defend herself. Her gaze locked on the handgun and then shot to the person holding it.

Kurtis Ferguson.

The sight was familiar. Memories poured through her mind in rapid succession, as if a key had twisted in the lock of an overflowing trunk. Dark rage clouded the edges of Felicity's vision. "It was you. You killed Brooke."

TWENTY-FOUR

Kurtis smirked. "I see your memories have finally returned. They say later is better than never, but in your case, I don't think that's true." He leveled the gun to her chest. "Drop the bat."

"Or what? You'll kill me? I'm sure that's the plan anyway." Felicity's mind whirled as she struggled to put the pieces together. There were holes she could only make educated guesses about. "You and Melanie are the leaders of Triple 6. You've been working together for a long time. Since before Brooke's murder. What happened, Kurtis? Did she uncover what you were doing and confront you?" It fit with her memories. Felicity's gaze flickered to Daniel, who struggled to his feet. "She knew you'd involved her brother and was angry."

"Yes. Initially, she thought it was just me, but then my industrious ex-girlfriend discovered that Melanie had created fake bank accounts using Brooke's credentials. She confronted me while I was there picking up my stuff.

Told me to stop using her name and involving her brother or she'd go to the police."

"Jeremy overheard your conversation while fixing the gutters." Felicity's heart broke for the man. He'd probably been keeping watch over Brooke's house from his parents'. Jeremy had known she was in trouble. "You came back later that night. What did you tell Brooke to get her to open the door?"

"That I'd forgotten something."

Just as Felicity had suspected. "The argument between the two of you kicked off again. I overheard part of it. Brooke kept saying you can't do this." She stared at the horrible man holding her at gunpoint. "She loved you. And Melanie. She understood the magnitude of what you two were doing and wanted to give you an opportunity to get out of the drug business before the police got involved. You used her kindness against her."

Kurtis shrugged. "She was stupid. Melanie and I were making a fortune. Neither of us were interested in giving it up."

He'd shot her instead. Felicity heard it, came downstairs, and found Brooke's body. Jeremy must've also seen or heard something because he came in the back door. There was a noise in the rear bedroom. Jeremy gripped Felicity's shoulders and told her to hide. She'd run upstairs to the closet. "You were looking for something in Brooke's bedroom. She had proof, didn't she?"

"Records I found and destroyed." Kurtis glowered. "My only mistake was leaving you and Jeremy alive. I didn't realize either of you were in the house until the next day. Jeremy wasn't too much of a concern. The police knew he was crazy. But you... I nearly killed you too, but your dad cleared out of town and I figured the whole thing was done."

"Until I came back and reopened the case."

Kurtis glanced at Daniel. "Tie her up and then get the truck ready. I want the police searching for her body for a while."

They were going to kill her and dump her some place in the woods. Felicity shifted in preparation to resist, but then Kurtis shifted his gun to Harper, who was still lying on the carpet. "I don't want to shoot this child, but I will do what is necessary to get your cooperation."

His tone was deadly serious. Felicity dropped the bat.

Daniel punched her in the face and stars exploded across her vision. Blood filled her mouth. Rough hands grabbed her wrists and pulled them behind her. Felicity put all her focus on bending her elbows to create a wide gap. Daniel zip-tied her hands together.

She spat a mix of saliva and blood onto the carpet. DNA. Noah and Grady would eventually find this place. They'd know she'd been there.

Daniel collected the bat from the floor and raised it, preparing to hit her. His pupils were pinpricks. Felicity realized he was high. He hadn't been arrested for possession in a long time but clearly was still using. Fear shot straight through her. She wouldn't be able to defend herself against an attack from a bat with her hands tied.

"Don't." Kurtis's tone was sharp.

Daniel whirled to face him. "You said I could have some fun."

His boss shot him a disgusted look. "That was before she beat you up. Again." He glanced at his watch. "We don't have time for any more delays. Get the van. Now."

Daniel hesitated and then left the room. Felicity let go of the breath she was holding but kept her senses sharp. She was a long way from being out of danger. Harper too. "It's not smart to have a drug user on the payroll."

To her surprise, Kurtis laughed. "You're right. It's not. Daniel doesn't normally handle this side of the business." He leveled the gun on her again. "But it's an all-hands-on-deck situation now."

Felicity glared up at Kurtis. "What are you going to do with Harper?"

"I'll make sure she's found." He shrugged. "Law enforcement comes out in full force when a kid gets hurt. I've poked that bear enough. Besides, I don't enjoy killing unless I have to."

"Nice to know there are some lines you don't cross." Felicity didn't believe one word Kurtis uttered. He'd kill Harper in a heartbeat. She spat more blood into the carpet and then rolled over to push herself into a sitting position to face Kurtis. Had she left enough gap in the zip tie? She attempted to tug her hand free, but her knuckle snagged against the plastic.

"Why all the games? You want me dead." A thought formed in her mind, and she inhaled sharply. "You're buying time. Creating situations so the police are spread thin and don't have time to uncover your crimes. Where's Melanie? She's erasing the bank records, isn't she?"

It was the only thing that made sense. Laundering money left a paper trail, and as the bank manager, Melanie had access to these records remotely. Noah had been right. The leader—no, leaders—of Triple 6 were cleaning house. Kurtis and Melanie were working off a plan. Once they erased any sign of their involvement, Melanie would be "found" or "escape" the clutches of the "killers." She'd be viewed as a victim. No one would question her involvement.

Except... she'd been caught on video kidnapping Harper. Felicity's gaze narrowed. "Does Melanie know you plan to kill her once she's erased the records that connect you to Triple 6?"

He smirked again. "You talk too much."

"What about Daniel? Does he know you're going to frame him for all of this?" She wriggled her hand as much as possible without drawing Kurtis's attention. "This property is connected to him, isn't it? I bet he doesn't know you left Jeremy's body in his garage or that the police have been searching for him since yesterday."

Her hand popped free. Relief flooded through her, but she was careful to keep it off her expression. "My guess is Gene is already dead. You got rid of him after the bank bombing. You'll use Daniel to help kill me, then set him up for Melanie's murder, too, so it'll look like Melanie and Daniel were working together to run Triple 6."

"Shut up." Kurtis bent down to take her arm, shoving

the gun under her chin. The barrel pressed against her skin. Cold and deadly. "No more talking or I'll blow your head off right here." He glanced at the doorway, presumably to make sure Daniel hadn't overheard their conversation, and then focused back on her. The malevolence in his eyes was bone-chilling. "You've caused me enough trouble. One more peep out of you about this and I'll make sure Harper pays for it. You got me?"

She let the fear cramping her insides show on her expression. The more Kurtis believed he was in control, the less he would expect her next move. "Yes."

He removed the gun from under her chin. Felicity balled her hand into a fist and leaned back so Kurtis would have to pitch forward more to yank her from the carpet. He glanced at the doorway again and then gripped her arm tighter. "Let's go."

He shifted his body weight forward in preparation to lean back and pull.

She socked him in the face and then flipped his body over hers. Kurtis landed on his back, stunned. Felicity didn't waste a second. She knocked the gun from his hand. He rose, attempting to grab her, and she scrambled away. A well-placed kick landed right in his face. Bone and cartilage gave way.

Kurtis screamed as blood erupted from his nose. He instinctively grabbed at his face with both hands. Felicity scooped Harper from the floor, pressing the baby against her chest, and bolted from the room.

Escape. She had seconds to escape.

The hallway emptied into a living room, the kitchen

beyond it. The back door gaped open like a beacon. She raced for it. The front door creaked open, followed by Daniel's shout. Felicity gripped Harper tighter. She added more fuel to her legs.

Rain pelted her skin as she flew across the yard. The shelter of the forest was a dozen steps away. Felicity heard Kurtis yelling. He and Daniel were coming for her. For her and Harper. Thunder rumbled like a bad omen. Her focus locked on an opening in the overgrowth. She had to make it there. Had to hide.

She stumbled over a root. Her knees hit the ground with bone-jarring pain, and she nearly dropped the precious bundle in her arms. Something whizzed past her and embedded in the tree branch above her head. They were shooting at her.

Felicity got back on her feet, moving in a zigzag pattern to make her figure harder to hit. Bark exploded as she passed a pine tree. The echo of a gunshot filled her ears. She flinched, stifling a scream.

And kept running.

TWENTY-FIVE

Lightning lit up the sky as Grady slammed on the brakes near a muddy road leading into the woods. Noah hopped out, rain pelting his clothes and skin, to place a flag on the road. More officers and sheriff's deputies were en route. Marking the turn onto the property cost precious seconds—time Noah wasn't sure his daughter and Felicity had—but not doing so could mean backup wouldn't find the right place. He would risk his own life, but not Grady's. The Texas Ranger had a wife and two kids to get home to.

Noah hopped back inside the vehicle. Grady handed him a bulletproof vest before slipping on his own. Each of them was armed with handguns and rifles. They had no idea what they were about to face. Triple 6 was a widespread criminal organization. It wouldn't be too much of a stretch to believe this land was protected by several individuals.

Grady punched the gas, his tires spraying mud

behind them. He navigated through bumps and ruts without hitting the brakes. His truck was powerful. The engine revved as tree branches threatened to close in on them.

Noah gripped his rifle in one hand and the handle over the door with the other. "If this goes south, get out, Grady. I mean it."

"Not a chance." Grady growled and gripped the steering wheel, never taking his eyes from the road. "Felicity is one of ours. And that's your daughter in there. No one comes after us and gets away with it. No one."

His attitude wasn't something new. Members of law enforcement were a family. It got messy at times, but they'd walk through danger to help each other. Company A—Felicity's group of Texas Rangers—were particularly close. They supported and cared for each other in good times and protected each other in bad. Noah shared the same bond with the members of his department. Tucker, Jax, and several other officers were racing to the property at that very moment.

Would they get there in time? Noah didn't know.

The trees parted, and a house appeared. The truck from the church parking lot sat close to the forest. A white nondescript delivery van was near the front door. Gunshots erupted on the property. Noah didn't wait for the vehicle to come to a stop. He leapt from the truck and bolted across the yard to the house. His boots pounded against the slick grass. Rain fell into his eyes. Noah ignored it all, his sole focus on getting to Felicity and his daughter.

He burst through the open front door. Movement out back caught his attention. He spotted a flash of brunette hair a second before Felicity ducked into the woods. Noah might've been imagining things, but he could've sworn she was carrying Harper in her arms. Two men were chasing her.

Daniel and another man. Noah's pulse shot into the stratosphere when recognition hit him.

Kurtis Ferguson.

Noah raced to the back door, raising his rifle. "Police! Freeze!"

Daniel whipped around and fired. Bullets shredded the side of the building. Noah hit the deck, taking cover behind the wall. His breath came in pants. He belly-crawled to the doorway and steadied his rifle. Daniel had dipped behind a rusted-out tractor. He'd been holding a handgun, which had a limited number of bullets, but that didn't mean much. He could have an extra magazine.

Kurtis was gone. He'd disappeared into the woods in pursuit of Felicity and Harper. Noah was desperate to go after the man but couldn't cross the yard without risking Daniel killing him.

"It's over." Noah shouted. "Drop your weapon and come out with your hands up!"

Silence came in response. Then Daniel said, "I won't surrender."

"You're surrounded." Grady yelled from the side of the house. He must've gone around the building while Noah went through. Smart man. "There's only one way you walk out of the situation alive. Be smart, Daniel. Drop your weapon and come out with your hands up."

Noah kept his gun trained on the tractor, holding his breath. Rain and sweat dripped off his forehead. His heart was with Felicity and Harper in the woods, every second fearful that Kurtis would find and kill them, but he forced his attention on Daniel.

Trust in God. The words Felicity had spoken during their last conversation before everything went haywire replayed in Noah's memory. He would trust. He would have faith. God had given him Felicity and Harper. They were gifts. Precious gifts. But neither of them belonged to Noah. They were God's and He, in His ultimate wisdom, would watch over them. Right now, Noah's job was to watch Grady's back.

Movement showed Daniel was doing something. A gun flew over the side of the tractor, landing in the grass. "I'm putting up my hands. Don't shoot."

Noah didn't relax a muscle. This could be a trick.

Daniel's hands appeared above the tractor. Then he stepped free of the farm equipment into the open. Noah breathed out. "Hands on your head. Drop to your knees."

The criminal did as he was told. Noah rose, still keeping Daniel in his sights.

Grady approached with caution. "On the ground, face-first." When he'd done as ordered, Grady grabbed Daniel's wrists and cuffed him. He glanced up at Noah. "I've got this. Go."

Noah bolted for the woods. Gunshots erupted, breaking the silence and sending his heart skittering. No.

No. No. He used the sound to guide his movements, heading straight for the danger. A flash of color caught his attention. Kurtis. Noah slowed and circled closer. Where were Felicity and Harper? There was no sign of them.

Sirens wailed. Backup was here.

Noah used the sound to cover his approach. Kurt was moving randomly, as if searching for something. For Felicity? It was likely. Hopefully, she'd find a hiding place with Harper. Blood coated Kurtis's face and his eyes were swelling. A broken nose. Felicity must've given him that, and despite the worry deep in his bones, a twinge of pride cut through Noah. He picked up his pace behind the criminal. It wouldn't take long for the police to flood these woods.

Rain pelted Noah's skin. His clothes were soaked, his hair wet. Water dripped in his eyes and the ground was slippery. He didn't care. Kept moving. As long as Kurt was in his sights, then the man couldn't hurt Felicity or Harper. He kept tracking him. Where was the backup?

At some point, Kurtis bent over at the waist. His breath was coming in short bursts. Noah took the opportunity to make his move. He shifted behind the man and held the rifle to the back of Kurtis's head. "Drop it."

Kurtis hesitated. For a heartbeat, Noah feared the man would ignore his order and attack.

Then Tucker stepped out of the shadow of a tree, gun raised. The former Army Ranger's footsteps had been silent as he'd tracked them in the woods. "I'd listen to him if I were you."

The gun hit the earth. Tucker lifted his gaze to

Noah's and then shifted to communicate that he would secure Kurtis. "Hands on your head."

Again, Kurt complied. Noah kept his gun trained on him until Tucker had him secure. Once the deed was done, he lowered his rifle. "I'm going in search of Felicity."

"It's too late." Kurt glowered. Hatred poured from every inch of his body as Tucker hauled him to his feet. "They're dead."

Noah's world tilted as the ground underneath him swayed. The gunshots. But Kurt had been searching the woods... "You're lying."

He grinned triumphantly, the expression horrifying with all the blood coating his face. Kurt met Noah's gaze. "No, I'm not. You'll see."

TWENTY-SIX

Felicity opened her eyes. Sunlight filtered through the panes on the window to create shapes on the hospital floor. A set of boots extended from the chair next to her bed. She trailed her gaze up the long legs and across the broad chest to Noah's gorgeous face. His eyes were closed, but one hand cupped hers. Even in his sleep, he was watching over her. She smiled. Thankful prayers lifted from her heart for the gift of another day with the man she loved.

"Hey." Noah sat up, blinking the sleep from his eyes. He gently squeezed her hand. "How are you feeling?"

"Better."

The emergency room doctor had insisted on keeping her overnight for observation. Felicity had taken several knocks to the head in the last few days, and her body was bruised and battered from being hit with the baseball bat. Thankfully, no bones were broken, although she sliced her leg pretty badly on a rock while running from Kurtis in the woods. It'd taken a dozen stitches to put her back together.

Harper was completely untouched. She'd slept through the whole incident and woke up after they reached the hospital in her father's arms. Something else Felicity was grateful for. "How's Harper?"

"She's fine. The doctor said the drug they used to sedate her has completely cleared her system. She won't have any adverse side effects." Noah reached for a carafe of water and a cup as she raised the bed to a sitting position. He poured some water and handed it to her.

She sipped slowly through the straw, the cool liquid coursing down her throat and soothing her dry mouth. She leaned against the pillow. "Did you stay all night?"

"You didn't think I was going to let you out of my sight for a moment, did you? Not after that stunt you pulled." He kissed her forehead to take the sting from his words. "You scared me, Fee. Promise you won't ever do that again."

"I'm sorry." She took his hand. His request wasn't unfair. She'd ignored her training and acted recklessly by going after Harper on her own. Felicity hadn't seen any other option at the time though. "All I could think about was Harper."

"I know." His gaze was tender. "I suppose I can't be too mad since you saved her life." This time, his kiss landed on her lips. As gentle as a butterfly wing, and fleeting, but with so much passion and tenderness, it brought tears to her eyes.

Noah swiped at one as it coursed down her cheek.

"Once Daniel found out that Kurtis had set him up to take the fall for everything, he spilled his guts. If you hadn't followed their instructions and gone to the farm, the plan was to murder Harper." Anger flared in his expression. "Kurtis wanted to break you. And me. He hoped Harper's death would keep us from pursuing Brooke's murder and the Triple 6 any further."

"Stupid plan."

"Agreed. He was desperate to buy time so Melanie could erase the bank records. Grady arrested her within an hour of Kurtis. Neither of them will see the outside of a prison cell. Ever." He sighed. "Although there may be a trial. Trials, actually. Neither of them confessed and have lawyered up. You may have to testify."

She ran her fingers over the warm skin along his knuckles. "It won't be the first time I've faced down killers in court. I'm not afraid." Felicity frowned. "So Kurtis and Melanie were running Triple 6?"

"Not exactly. They're part of the organization, and had a lot of territory here in Knoxville, but they aren't completely in charge. They operated more like a franchise. Grady is going to continue working the case over the next few months. It'll take time to track all the money that transferred hands through Knoxville Bank, but he hopes it'll lead to everyone involved in Triple 6. We want to shut it down. For good."

Felicity would request to assist on the case. Her boss might not agree, but it was worth asking. She blew out a breath. "One thing I can't understand is why Kurtis did it. He comes from money."

"His dad apparently had a gambling problem and blew through most of the family's fortune. Kurtis started selling drugs after law school. With his connections, Triple 6 leadership moved him up higher in the ranks. Then he got Melanie involved. Working together, I guess, created a bond. He dumped Brooke and started dating Melanie."

"What a love story." Her nose wrinkled. "Kurtis planned to kill her."

"According to Daniel, he'd grown tired of the marriage and wanted an out. Melanie didn't know what his plan was, so when he convinced her to kidnap Harper in order to create a distraction so she could finish covering their trail, she agreed."

"What about shooting her at the bank?"

"An accident. Since the wound was superficial, Daniel stitched her up."

Felicity frowned. "How did Daniel manage to hide his drug activity for so long? He was high when he attacked me at the house."

"Daniel worked for Kurtis before Brooke's death, but then got sober. Triple 6 wouldn't let him out of the business all together however. Kurtis and Melanie paid him to stay quiet while they used bank accounts in his name to launder money." Noah shook his head. "Daniel suspected Kurtis had killed Brooke, but wasn't angry about it since he'd told his sister to stay out of things."

"Wow." Felicity couldn't comprehend the callousness.

"Yeah. After Gene failed to kill you a few times,

Kurtis got Daniel involved. They needed his help to pull off the attack at the bank. He started using again. After Melanie was shot, Kurtis flipped out. He was furious they'd come close to killing her before she had the chance to wipe the records. He shot Gene. We found the man's body in the woods near the house you and Harper were held in."

No one deserved to be murdered, but Felicity wasn't going to lose sleep over the criminal's death. She sighed. "You know if a respected criminal judge and a bank manager were involved in Triple 6, we can't discount anyone. It's frightening how many people may be a part of the organization and the lengths they may go to. Kurtis lied to everyone right up to the very end." She squeezed his hand. "I can't imagine what it must've been like for you when he said Harper and I were dead."

Guilt pricked her. Kurtis had known exactly the right nerve to hit. It'd taken another twenty minutes for Noah to find Felicity and Harper. If the roles had been reversed, it would've been the worst twenty minutes of her life. "I'm so sorry."

"You have nothing to apologize for." Noah lifted her hand to his mouth and brushed her knuckles with his lips. "I'm thankful you and Harper are okay. We have a lot to be grateful for."

"You can say that again."

He reached for a bakery bag on the nightstand and opened it. The scent of warm sugar and blueberries wafted out. "Cassie came by earlier to check on you. She brought breakfast." He handed her a muffin with a crunchy streusel topping.

Felicity's stomach growled. She took a bite and sighed with pleasure. "Now all I need is some coffee."

Noah's cell phone dinged, and he grinned. "It's on the way. Aunt Imogene, Uncle Sam, Amber, and Harper are in the elevator."

Moments later, Noah's family poured into the room. Felicity's heart expanded at the sight of them, but her gaze shot straight to Harper, who was dressed in cute shorts and a tiger T-shirt. The little one shot straight across the room with a broad smile on her face. Noah had been right. She was fine. Thank God.

"Fee!" Harper squealed with excitement and attempted to climb on the bed.

Her curls bounced when Noah lifted her into his arms. "Fee has some boo-boos. Be gentle, okay?"

"Okay." She grinned back, her dimples flashing.

Felicity held out her arms and Noah deposited Harper next to her. She wrapped the child in an embrace and kissed the top of her head, breathing in her baby scent. Love swelled inside her, bigger than anything she could've imagined. Then her gaze snagged Noah's. Tears shimmered in his eyes. It caused a lump in her throat.

Imogene kissed her cheek. "How are you feeling, sweetie?"

"Much better, thanks."

"We brought you some coffee." Amber came forward to hand Felicity a takeaway cup. A shy smile graced the teenager's face. "I wasn't sure how you liked it, so I told them black. Cousin Noah says all cops drink their coffee black."

Felicity laughed. "Black is perfect."

Chief Garcia wore a wrinkled uniform and a five-o'clock shadow coated his jawline. He patted Noah on the shoulder in a manly greeting. "I've been up all night processing the paperwork and listening in on Daniel's confession. We have a lot to discuss, but we can do that over the next few days." Sam offered a tired smile. "Grady and Tucker are eager to see you. I told them it might be better to wait until this afternoon. Let you get some more rest before the entire group descends on you."

Imogene laughed. "Actually, it might be easier to have a gathering at my house with everyone. Jason and Nathan have been calling to check on you, too, along with their wives. We can do it in a couple of days. Unless..." Her voice trailed off. "You don't think you'll be feeling up to it."

"I'll be fine." She sipped her coffee. Harper spotted the muffin on the table over the bed, and realizing she wanted some, Felicity broke off a piece and handed it to her. "But I don't want to put you out."

"Nonsense. I love having people over." She patted Felicity's foot. "After you're released from the hospital, you're coming to the ranch to spend a few days and recuperate. We're going to make sure you get lots of R&R." She pinned her with a look. "Not one word otherwise, missy. We're so grateful—" Her voice choked up. Sam placed a hand on his sister's shoulder in silent comfort, and Imogene laughed. "My emotions are running away with me. Anyway, we're grateful all of you are okay. It's something to celebrate."

Warmth flooded Felicity's chest. "I'd love that."

"Okay, then." She clapped her hands together. "Well, we don't want to overtire you." Imogene frowned. "Harper, honey, you've gotten crumbs all over the bed."

Harper giggled. Felicity shook out the sheets and planted another kiss on the little girl's head. "That's all right. I like crumbs. Want some more muffin?"

"More, more, more!" She bounced with each word, and the mattress rattled Felicity's body. Her stitches pulled on the swollen and tender skin on her leg.

Felicity tried to hide her wince, but Noah immediately picked up on it. He scooped up his daughter and smothered her in kisses and tickles. "I think it's time you say bye to Fee. You can come back later to see her."

Harper waved, her innocent smile reaching inside Felicity's chest and squeezing her heart hard. She waved back. "Bye, honey. See you soon."

The group left. Noah shut the door behind them and came back to her bedside. "You okay? Need some pain meds?"

"Nope." She snagged his hand. "But I wouldn't say no to a kiss."

He didn't disappoint, sweeping down to capture her lips with his. Everything faded. The beep of the hospital equipment, the pain in her leg, and the feel of the mattress underneath her body. Nothing mattered except this strong, wonderful man and the feelings he created inside her. Felicity kissed him back with all the passion in her heart. When Noah finally pulled away, they were both breathless.

"Fee..." He cupped her face with his palm. His fingers dipped into her hair and a delicious sensation traveled down her neck and into her core. "We promised to go slowly. And we will, but you should know my intentions. One day, I want to make you my wife. I hope that doesn't scare you."

"It doesn't scare me. We should give Harper some time to get used to the idea of us, and I need to work on figuring out a work-life balance, but nothing would make me happier than to be Mrs. Felicity Hodge." She met his gaze. She saw forever in his eyes. "I love you, Noah."

"I love you too."

TWENTY-SEVEN

Nine months later

A cloud shifted in the bluebird sky and sunshine streamed across the yard. Balloons danced in the breeze, attached to picnic tables covered with tablecloths. The sounds of kids screaming with delight drifted from the bouncy house near the fence line. The scent of hamburgers and hotdogs scented the air. Guests mingled around, talking and laughing. Country music poured from the speakers strategically placed for the best sound quality.

Noah wrapped an arm around Felicity's waist and pulled her to his side. Her hair tumbled around her shoulders in tightly wound curls and a beautiful flush colored her cheeks. She was stunning. His heart stuttered as he brushed a kiss across her lips. "The party is a huge success. Harper is having the best time."

"Well, you only turn three once."

As if called by their conversation, Harper busted out of the bouncy house and bolted across the grass on bare feet. Noah's little girl had grown up so much over the last year. Smart and healthy, with more opinions than ever. It brought a smile to his face. He figured his little one would always be strong willed.

"Fee!" She tackled Felicity, who'd bent down to be on Harper's level, nearly bowling the gorgeous woman over with the force of her embrace. "I jumped the highest. I almost touched the sky!"

"Wow."

"Come see me!" She wriggled away just far enough to grab Felicity's hand. Then paused. "When do we get cake?"

Felicity laughed. "Soon. Go ahead to the bouncy house and I'll join you in a minute. I want to talk to your dad."

"Okay!"

She raced across the yard again. Noah watched with his mouth open. "I was standing right here, and she didn't even give me the time of day. It's all Fee this and Fee that." His tone was light so Felicity would know he was teasing. Nothing brought him more joy than seeing how much his daughter got along with his fiancée.

Noah lifted Felicity's hand to his lips. Her engagement ring sparkled in the sunshine. "Have you decided on a date for our big day?"

"Actually, that's what I wanted to talk to you about." She wrapped her arms around his waist. "What do you say to a small ceremony in the church next month with just close family? Then we can do a big reception like this one in Imogene's yard to celebrate."

Noah would be happy with anything as long as Felicity was his wife. "Are you sure you don't want a big wedding?" It would be her first marriage and he wanted to do right by her. "I don't want you to have any regrets."

"What I want is to marry you. No matter how we do it, there will never be any regrets." She squeezed his waist. "But I love the idea of a country reception. Good food, great music, and simple attire. It fits who we are."

"It does. Word of warning though. Harper's expecting a princess dress."

Felicity laughed. "Oh, I know. She's already mentioned it a dozen times." Her eyes sparkled with happiness. "I can't wait to call you my husband. I love you, Noah."

"Love you too." He bent his head and kissed her. Over the last nine months, their relationship had only grown deeper and more powerful. Noah loved her more today than he had yesterday, which was saying something. But no matter how often they kissed, the woman still could reach right into his chest and grab hold of his heart.

Propriety had him ending the kiss long before he wanted to. Noah rested his forehead briefly against hers. "How long is this party again? I want to know when I can get you alone."

"For shame, Hodge." She laughed and lightly smacked his arm.

He chuckled at the blush rising in her cheeks and then lightly kissed her again. "You can't blame a man for wanting to be alone with the woman he loves."

"I suppose not." She grinned and then wriggled from his grasp. "I'd better check on Harper before she screams my name from inside the bouncy house." Her gaze drifted across the yard. "Oh, wait. There's Jason and Addison. Let's go say hello really quick."

Noah took her hand, and they crossed to the couple who'd just arrived. Jason carried several boxes in his hands, his German shepherd, Connor, keeping pace next to him. Addison, Jason's wife, greeted them with a wave. Her hair was tied back into a braid, and she had a baby carrier strapped to her chest. The couple's son, three-month-old Jackson, was sleeping peacefully. His dark hair waved in the breeze.

Felicity cooed. "Oh my goodness, look at how big he's gotten. Addison, what are you feeding him?"

"Just breastmilk, although he eats all day and all night. At this rate, I should be banging into the walls from lack of sleep. That's why we're late. I made the mistake of taking a nap and slept a lot longer than I meant to."

"You needed the rest." Jason gazed lovingly at his wife and son.

"Of course you did." Felicity smiled. "And you're not late at all. There's still plenty of food, thank goodness." She arched her brows. "Between the guys from the police department, the Texas Rangers in my company, and the Special Forces members, we're lucky to have anything left."

Addison laughed, her cheeks smushing with the effort. "Oh I know. Feeding this crowd takes a lot."

Jason lifted the boxes in his hand. "I brought something to help. Pies from Nelson's Diner. Best dessert this side of the Mississippi."

Noah had heard of the diner but hadn't been. He took the boxes from Jason's hands. "Thanks. That's mighty kind of you."

"Our pleasure."

"FEE!" Harper's tiny voice carried across the yard. Her head poked out of the zippered entrance to the bouncy house and she screamed again, "FEE!"

"That's my signal." Felicity laughed. "I knew she was going to do that."

She and Addison headed over to the bouncy house together. They were joined by Leah and Cassie. Like Addison, Cassie had her daughter tucked in a sling. Sophia, Leah's daughter, was jumping in the bouncy house.

Jason spotted Nathan and Tucker manning the grill and deviated in that direction. Noah carried the pie boxes to the dessert table. He set them down and opened the top one. The smell of apples and cinnamon wafted from the box. The crust was a perfect golden brown, the filling visible through the lattice work, gooey. "Wow."

"Whatcha got there?" Detective Jax Taylor appeared at his side. The lawman looked relaxed in faded blue jeans and a ball cap. He leaned over to glance inside the box and whistled. "Holy smokes, that's a pie from Nelson's? Okay, where are the plates? I've heard amazing things about this place but have never eaten there. It's in the middle of nowhere."

"It's off that old country road heading out of town, right?"

"Yep. The outside looks dodgy, but several people have said the food is amazing and the pies are the best in Texas."

"Let's find out." Noah hunted up some plates and silverware. He sliced into the apple pie and gave a hearty piece to Jax before helping himself. The moment the first bite hit his tongue, he groaned with pleasure. "Oh man. That is good."

He tipped up the other lids on the rest of the bakery boxes. "Looks like we've got pecan, chocolate walnut, some kind of strawberry thing, and a peach. Jason and Addison went all out."

Jax patted his stomach. "Thank goodness I left plenty of room for dessert." He glanced at Felicity and then lowered his voice. "Hey, man, I meant to ask. How is Felicity doing since the Ferguson trials? I know testifying can dredge up a lot of stuff."

"She's doing good. I am too." Kurtis and Melanie Ferguson were convicted on all counts and sentenced to life in prison without the possibility of parole. Daniel pled guilty, so there was no trial for him, and he also got a life sentence. Since he agreed to testify against Kurtis and Melanie, the prosecutor agreed to a potential parole. But that was a long way off. The man would probably spend the next forty years or so in prison. "Knowing Kurtis and Melanie won't ever be able to hurt anyone is comforting."

Investigations into Triple 6 were still ongoing. Uncovering the identities of the organization's leadership would take time.

Jax's gaze snagged on something and his expression darkened. "What's she doing here?"

Noah was caught off-guard by the hostility in his colleague's tone. Jax was laidback and easygoing even in stressful situations. "Who?"

"Megan Ingles." He gestured to a blonde woman in a green dress standing near the bouncy house.

"Oh. Megan and Felicity attend bible study together." Noah frowned. "I'm pretty sure Megan is also a friend of Leah's. She's a therapist, if I remember correctly. Do you know her?"

"Yep." His mouth pulled tight and his shoulders were stiff. "She killed my brother."

ALSO BY LYNN SHANNON

Texas Ranger Heroes Series

Ranger Protection

Ranger Redemption

Ranger Courage

Ranger Faith

Ranger Honor

Ranger Justice

Ranger Integrity

Ranger Loyalty

Ranger Bravery

Ranger Purpose

Triumph Over Adversity Series

Calculated Risk

Critical Error

Necessary Peril

Strategic Plan

Covert Mission

Tactical Force

Badge of Honor Series

Fractured Memories

Dangerous Lies

Would you like to know when my next book is released? Or when my novels go on sale? It's easy. Subscribe to my newsletter at www.lynnshannon.com and all of the info will come straight to your inbox!

Reviews help readers find books. Please consider leaving a review at your favorite place of purchase or anywhere you discover new books. Thank you.

Made in the USA
Columbia, SC
05 January 2025

51267316R00126